CASSIUS

The Wild Flower Series 3

RACHELLE MILLS

Cassius

Limitless Publishing, LLC
Kailua, HI 96734
www.limitlesspublishing.com

Formatting: Limitless Publishing

ISBN-13: 978-1-64034-788-5

DEDICATION

To the Wildflowers...

PROLOGUE

Blue Memories

Cassius

A trace of fresh paint still clings to the walls.

Kennedy sits in the rocker with her back to me.

"It's finished." The words are blown out slowly from her chest—she continues to rock with her head resting on the back of the chair, looking at the mural she painted of me as the leader wolf of a made-up pack.

"Do you need anything? I was going to make something to eat."

She silently shakes her head no.

Walking towards her, there's a hesitation before I place a hand on her shoulders—she flinches.

Not once did she ever recoil from him.

Concentrating on biting my tongue, I hold my thoughts from her. I focus on the silhouette of two people holding hands walking into the evening sun.

"What's that?" Walking to the image, I point a

finger at the drawing.

"A dream," she murmurs without looking into my eyes.

"Here." I stretch my hand for her to take the cup of tea. "I put fresh mint in it."

She doesn't glance at me when she takes the first sip, only at the dream where my finger was at.

Do I want to scream *what dream*? Is it him or me? I choose to swallow down the scream and walk away.

"I'm sorry, Cassius." Her voice hits me softly before I step out of the room.

"Why are you sorry, Kennedy?"

"That I'm not what you wanted for a mate." Her voice seems flat.

Dust filters through the air from the partially open blinds. Everything feels covered in something thick and heavy.

"You're what I wanted—it was him that I didn't expect to have with us." Her shoulders sag into the wooden rocking chair, body slumping.

I can feel her ache—I can feel my own ache.

Love is a cruelty that aches us in all directions—except together.

Kennedy stands slowly, arching her back before righting herself on thin legs—her collarbone juts out sharply. She's all skin that's stretched tight over bones. Dark shadows swallow the color of her eyes.

Dry, cracked lips press together without a smile. Mine press together, tight and unforgiving.

This is in-between. No words uttered, but we both need to scream. I can feel her voice raging within her chest, and I can feel mine trying to come out as hard as the earlier days with her.

"Are you ready to go?"

"I'm ready." She looks around the room, verifying that the cribs have been set up. The mural consumes every inch of space on the walls from ceiling to baseboards.

A sound escapes through her hard-pressed lips. A small cry.

"I'm afraid." Her hands go over the futures that are nesting inside her. A boy, a girl.

"You're going to be fine. They will be fine. We are going to be fine." She doesn't flinch this time when my hands go on either side of her shoulders. I do it slowly, cautiously. Her chin tilts up, and I get to see her up close. I want to kiss her. I don't.

"You're going to be a good father." Her fingertips press into the base of my spine.

"You're going to be a good mother."

Her lips press harder together, and her lids close. Not opening up. A tear escapes, along with a sob from a chest that is aching.

"Cassius—" She gives a deep pause.

"Yes, Kennedy."

"I want you to be happy if something happens to me. I want you to be happy and live a good life."

"Nothing will happen to you." I press my forehead to hers. "I'm happy."

"No, you're not. Neither am I. We both know it. We can't lie to each other. There is no more time for lies between us." Her sound is raw with undigested truthfulness; it breaks with its final note.

It's my turn to blink without opening my eyes back up. The smell of warm mint is on her breath.

3

There is no more time for silence; only our sound should be heard between the both of us.

"I'm not happy, not yet. I will be. I know it. We need time, Kennedy." Insatiable, the way the sound of silence is eaten away by rough words.

"I could have loved you, Cassius. I want you to know that."

"You still can," I beg her. The feeling of a knife blade skewers into the next beat of my heart, sharp, cruel. I grit my teeth against the pain.

"I can love you, Kennedy. I want you to know that. I want you to know that it's not too late for us. It's not over for us. We have our lives ahead of us. I can love you better than him. I know it." Peeling my own skin back, I expose myself to her in a clean cut.

"I know you could." The palm of her hand touches my cheek; our foreheads press harder together. We breathe together.

I want to kiss those pale lips and ghost-filled eyes. I want to show her real passion, real dedication. I want my name to coat her mouth. I want to show her everything all at once. I want, want, want…yet she doesn't hunger for my wants. It's more her sacrifice to love me. She's sacrificing her dreams, desires, for me.

I don't want to be her sacrifice.

"I was thinking after the twins are born, you could go to that art school you always wanted to go to. We could rent an apartment. Live in the city until you're done with school."

A brutal cry comes from deep in her chest. Her hand grips my neck harder. Not enough to leave bruises, she doesn't have that strength anymore.

A shallow breath in from her chest.

I'm clutching to hope.

Her eyes open wider, the widest I've ever seen them.

"You would do that?" A gnaw on her bottom lip. She's thinking. I love to watch her think when it comes to us.

"We would do that." Letting her know it's we. Life sparks up. Her eyes start to shine again, only briefly, before the fade returns. She smiles, but the curve of her lips drops at the edges.

Mint is breathed out slowly.

"I would like that."

"Me too." I'm smiling.

She shifts on her feet. "We should go." A grimace burrows deeper into the lines around her eyes.

"In the top drawer, there's a box for you, Cassius."

"What is it?"

"My life." A gnarled-up sound escapes from her tightening throat, her words barely squeezing out.

"A life in a box doesn't seem like a life at all." Trying to make things lighter. It doesn't work. She seems to be weighted down more than she already is.

"It's letters. I wrote to them, to you." Words cease after that; she's crying again. Shaking.

I shake with her. Holding her to me. She allows this.

"I'm so scared."

"I know you are, but nothing will happen to you. I promise you'll be fine. I'm going to be at your side the whole time."

She cries harder, staining my shirt in tears and snot. I'm afraid that even the act of crying is wearing her out too much. Her body is barely holding on to life.

A grunt comes from Kennedy, and she clutches her belly. "It's time, Cassius." Her eyes are wild, afraid. The *Wild* within the marrow of my bones rumbles his support. He makes it known he is here with her as well.

"It's time."

"Don't forget about the box." Her hand clutches my wrist, squeezing it.

"I won't forget, because you'll remind me. Let's go." Walking down the stairs, she takes them one at a time.

The ride to the clinic is fast. Tires grind along the asphalt road, everything passing in a blur.

Another grunt through teeth consumes the inside of the car. Calling my mother, I tell her it's time. I throw the phone as soon as the call is made.

"My parents are on their way."

Kennedy doesn't say a word. Her lips are still hard-pressed, and sweat beads at her temples, wetting her hair.

Once the car stops, I'm out and scoop Kennedy up in my arms. She's light, without any meat to cling on her bones. Fear creeps in, a whispering dark thought that this isn't going to go well cannibalizing all other good thoughts.

"We need help." I kick open the door. We are met with the midwife's eyes. They go big, but she's calm.

The clinic smells clean until a gush of blood comes from between my mate's legs. Kennedy gnashes her teeth from side to side. I hear the grind of them.

"Put her down here. I'm going to get the doctor." Laying her down on the bed, a wave of blood pushes outward, spilling on the floor. I can hear the drips leaking off the sheets. One drop after the other.

"Help us!" I scream. Both the doctor and the midwife come into the room. They look at each other. Grim-faced, hard as stone.

"Cassius…" Kennedy grips my hand. Our eyes lock onto each other as the doctor cuts the skirt and her underwear away from her body.

She takes in a breath; her face holds the pain.

The muscles of her body shake.

Kennedy arches her back upwards. A low moan trembles out of her half-open mouth. A cry leaves mine.

"We need the tray." Murmured words come out fast from a doctor who looks concerned.

"The tray?" The midwife holds her eyes to the doctor before she nods her head.

"What's going on?" I try to speak, try to hold Kennedy's hand, which has lost its grip on mine.

"We need to be prepared to take them out of her if she can't push them out." He's between her legs, and the midwife is now on the other side of Kennedy.

"We need you to try and push your babies out." His order comes out, short, crisp. The bed converts to a chair, the bottom sliding away. Kennedy's legs shake with the exertion to push.

"Look at me, Kennedy. You need to push them out of you." Wiping away her sweat, she's bitten her tongue, and her mouth fills with blood. Her teeth are stained red as she lifts her lips up, grunting with effort.

"I can't." Her head is shaking side to side.

"Yes, you can. Don't give up. Fight. Push them out of you." I want to scream except my lungs can't pull in enough air. I'm feeling strangled. She's losing her life in front of my eyes.

Blood on top of blood.

Her chest heaves. "Why did you turn off the lights?" A calm question comes from a mouth that is hanging open. Eyes dilating.

The bed eases down. She's no longer in a squatting position.

Everything blurs. It's too fast, too slow. I can't see because she is slipping away. I can see her fading light in my eyes. Through my vision. Even knees hitting the floor don't really register. My nose is pressed against her cheek. Eyes pinched shut.

"Do something!"

"They are." My mom's hands are on my shoulder.

I can't look at her. Only her voice breaks through my cries.

Her heart is racing, pounding in my ears. Thready, not normal.

"She's in v-fib."

"It's time." I can hear the scrape of silver against the metal tray. I press my lips to her ear.

"I love you." I repeat it to Kennedy over and

over again. She doesn't say it back. Her body relaxes.

My mother cries. Her hand never leaves my shoulder, squeezing while I'm tearing in half. No one tells me to stop shaking her. "Try harder! Fight for them!" I yell over and over again.

I don't open my eyes, even when her heart stops. I don't open my eyes when the first cries hit my ears, followed by another distinct cry. I rock her head in my hands, holding onto her until the warmth slips away. The mark on my neck ignites fire until that feeling is burned away. I don't get off my knees. I don't look, can't listen.

I just can't.

CHAPTER 1

Memories in the Color of Mint

Treajure

Whiskey blurs his sight.

Stumbling over his feet, Cassius makes his way over to the wall. He sways with hands dug deep into his pockets, looking at her picture.

A mouth full of mumbled apologies flare up into his fire. Sometimes his words are soaked in a red rage where anger runs rampant in his veins to greet her face. There are times when it's blue, and he chokes and drowns on his own tears, dropping to his knees before he wipes his eyes on the edge of his sleeve.

There are times he chooses to feed all the darkest of his demons. He thinks he's a monster; I think he's broken.

Sometimes memories are the color of mint: sweet, loving, but tones into jealousy. Why Cassius likes mint is confusing, because *he* never liked mint in his tea. That was one of the few things they never did together.

Staying quiet, I get to witness his confessions to the picture on the wall. Does he know I'm not deaf? Just voiceless.

"Specs, why aren't you sleeping?" A slight slur, hardly noticeable.

It's always one way between us. He asks the questions, and I listen. He will sometimes answer for me; only rarely does he ever answer his own questions. I prefer when he answers; that way there isn't anything left unanswered between us.

I know everything about Cassius Denver Valentine, and he knows everything he's already answered about me. I was raised in the Wilds of Valentine, where my voice was stolen by an evil jealous queen, but one day soon, he thinks the magic will come and let me talk once again. He likes to make up these magical stories when I sleep underneath his bed. So far everything he's made up about me has been wrong.

There is no belief in magic anymore. I thought playing pretend was over for me, but when I look at Cassius, I want to play pretend again. *Where he is the magic, and I'm his wish.*

Regarding the picture again, his hand pulls out from his deep pockets. Dry blood coats his fingers, and the dirt clings underneath his nails. There is a hint of mint below the whiskey of his breath.

He's been to the cemetery.

Kennedy's grave will never be forgotten by him. His wish would never be wasted on me.

"Why are you still up so late, Specs?" A shrug of

my shoulder. What I don't say is that I wanted to be here when you got home from the party. I know exactly where to sit to be discreetly away to give him space when he comes into this room to look at her, but when he turns, he'll see me. I want him to see me with my red earrings on.

"Couldn't sleep, could you? Me either." He's back at looking at her. Raising his hand again, almost to touch her face. Almost.

There's old blood on Cassius's hand. He won't pick up the twins when blood still clings to the webbing between his fingers. He won't let them see him with his own blood that sticks to him like a second skin. I see the blood. I always understand the blood. He doesn't care that I see it. For some reason, he doesn't hide it from me. Do I want to ask him why he must always bleed? I want to wash his blood from his hands, kiss his knuckles, and tell him you don't have to suffer to make yourself feel better. *You've already bled yourself enough.*

"I met someone tonight, Treajure." It's instant; my face feels shocking cold the way ice water feels when it's been splashed on my face. I could choke on my own icy shiver. Cassius seems to focus better now. His sway is steadier while a sway hits me. Fear chases at the beat of my heart. Pumping the blood in my ears, suffocating all other sounds away.

Do I want to ask who? I can't ask, preferring to stay entirely still. It's a balance to keep the quick shine out of my eyes and a sob from coming out the middle of my throat, but then again—I've had practice with keeping all my sounds silent.

"She reminds me of Kennedy." His eyes seem

12

love-starved. "Her name's Hazel." I start to taste something bitter, not the mint his breath holds. "She thinks I'm homeless." He gives a small laugh as he scratches at his beard that hasn't been trimmed in a while.

Turning from him, I can feel the way my top lip presses flat against the bottom lip. She wouldn't know but that's all of Cassius's layers, the hair, beard, several shirts, ring, watch, he uses layers to protect himself from the world.

"She's irritating." He goes on with things I have no interest in. "She has beautiful eyes." His voice lowers reverently. I have to push up my glasses that start to slip down the bridge of my nose.

Cassius steps closer to me before stumbling— long rough fingers curl around my waist. "Shhh," he says, with whiskey-minted breath to himself, because I didn't make the sound.

Sounds a dangerous thing...

The coarse hair on his face reminds me his soft lips are close to mine. The feeling of him this close will linger long after he's asleep. To him this is nothing. To me, it's everything.

Closing my eyes, I lean back slightly into him while he bends himself around my body.

"Are you going to try to sleep in your bed tonight, Specs?" He waits for a different answer than the one I always give him. I shake my head no.

He sighs. "One day you're going to have to sleep in your own bed and not underneath mine." My shoulders curl in from what he says. If I try to sleep in the bed they bought for me, I'll never sleep again. There's no safety on top of the bed, only underneath it. Cassius keeps me safe with his body over mine between the mattresses and wooden bed frame.

"I've met someone, Specs. Her eyes…" He says it like a prayer, but I feel the sin of this tragedy. Not the words I was expecting tonight. My mouth opens with wanting to say, "I'm happy for you," but I just can't get the sound out.

His chin rests on the edge of my shoulder. He's all brimstone and fire, and I'm, I'm the ash that's been left over from the way he burns through me.

Letter 1

Dear Cash,

Today is the first day I stopped hating you. I don't look at your face and hate it. I don't look at your hands and hate them.

I don't like you, but I don't hate you. The more I think about it, the more I feel sorry for you. You didn't really stand a chance with me. Not because you aren't strong, or capable, or anything else. You just aren't Clayton.

That's the sad fact. You could never be him, ever.

This isn't to make you feel bad, it probably will make you feel bad reading this, but I want you to understand me and understand why I can't love you the way you want me to accept and love you.

You did a lot of shitty things to me, Cash.

A lot.

You let your anger get the best of you, and you took it out on me. Me too. I let my anger get the best of me as well. I said and did some really shitty things to you. Really shitty things. You aren't a weak wolf. You aren't all those things that I yelled at you. I was just upset, just like you were upset. We were shit to each other.

Don't let your anger get the best of you. You're better than that. Remember that.

I hated you for a long time. I hated you touching me because I felt as if I was cheating on Clayton with how much I loved the way your skin feels on my skin. He tried to tell me about the mate bond when Rya came back, how he was trying to fight the pull. How when he looked at her, he felt as if he was cheating on me. I didn't understand what he was saying to me. I told him just don't look at her. He shook his head and told me he can't stop looking at her. I cried, and he held me and told me how sorry he was. He was trying to fight it, he was trying to fight the bond, but he felt himself losing himself to it.

I didn't understand how hard it was for him to fight for me, fight for us. He tried so hard, he tried so hard for me. And look at me.

I'm pregnant, not by him, but by you.

Now I know what he was feeling. I can't look away from you. I feel as if I am losing myself to the bond and that I am cheating on him. I feel guilty. I feel shame that I've only been with you for a small amount of time and I can't control myself around you. That all I want is to slide up against you, to have your arms hold me, let my cheek rest against your chest, but I still love Clayton.

I've stopped hating you, Cash. Today I've stopped hating you. Instead, I've started to hate myself for failing Clayton. All those years he fought against the bond for me and here I am with someone else's pups implanted deep in my belly.

You're my mate, but he's everything to me. Always will be.

So today is the day that I've stopped hating you. This isn't your fault. I blamed you. I blamed you for losing him. I blamed Rya for losing him. I blame the Moon for it all.

No one is to blame but me. I'm to blame, not anyone else.

I might not be able to love you, Cash, but I can't hate you either.

Kennedy.

CHAPTER 2

Mint turns into Wildflower Bruises

Waking up in a silent room is not something I like. For a moment, everything freezes into a stillborn breath.

Waiting. Waiting. Waiting.

Muscles start to seize up before they relax and realize I'm underneath the bed—not on top of one.

Cassius's discarded shirts are within reach. My fingers extend to pull the material to my nose like a sin. Inhaling like a true prayer.

My sanctuary in scent.

The fabric rubs between my fingers; the smell of him fills my pores. Shielded from prying eyes, inhaling again and again to make each breath count. Pretending it's his neck I have my nose against. My hand shoves down over the top of the material of my underwear. Fingers press, rub…not my fingers, but his. It's so easy to imagine. *To pretend…*

I'm not sure how I've gotten to this point, me under his bed touching myself when he leaves in the morning and pretending it's him. Before Cassius, I've never dreamed of wanting to touch myself, but with his scent wrapped around me, soft as a blanket in the quietest kind of strength, I'd let myself play pretend with the image of him.

The heat grows underneath the bed, throbbing heat, imagining his naked body, bare and pressed against mine. It's as if I can feel the weight of him. I want to make him moan the way I just did—all throat.

His shirt is in my mouth. I can taste him, teeth clamp down as my hand rubs between my legs, imagining it's his finger, thick and searching. The sensation is almost unbearable now. Biting down on the fabric. No noise.

Clutching my breast, squeezing the nipple until it hurts. Pain. This pain I crave. Shifting my legs, pushing into the slickness. Another low moan deep in my throat—eyes squeezed shut. I can see his face; it hovers above me. I'm making him shake the way my thighs are.

Moving my legs wider apart, letting out a hard breath.

Fingers tracing between my folds, pushing into the fabric before touching the spot that arches my back and demands to be rubbed faster, harder.

"Hmmm." The sound comes out with teeth clamped down on the material that smells of Cassius, that was against his bare chest. I can taste him…

Inside and out, the heat pulses. My pulse rages.

I can see Cassius in my mind; his eyes push my fingers faster, harder. The unbearable pleasure gaining strength. Trembling and twisting hips, arching back. My breast held tight by my own hand, pretending Cassius is the one palming it. It's enough for the pause, that beautiful moment where everything is still and nothing matters before the first hard clench of my inner walls release the breath that I was holding.

I come with his name on my lips, but the sound stuck in my throat.

I'm still biting the shirt as the gentle aftershocks of pulses wave through my core.

Clenching, unclenching until I can move from underneath the bed.

I smell of sex with myself, and I have to open the window and take his shirt and my things out of his room to go into mine.

My bed's made up perfectly; nothing is out of place. It seems too cold in here, not like Cassius's room that's the perfect temperature.

The blinds are drawn down. It's a shadowed room. Not meant for anything else but to hold my clothes. The Luna thought that if they made my room bright I'd sleep in the bed, if they darkened the room I'd sleep in the bed, had a TV, music, but nothing worked. I should have told them this, but I couldn't seem to get the words out that are stuck behind clenched teeth.

The day I fell asleep in the oatmeal is the day Cassius finally relented and let me sleep underneath his bed until my Belac comes back. He grumbled about how weird it was. How he's not going to be able to fall asleep, ever. I drifted off to him complaining underneath his breath. The first real sleep I had in seven days.

I knew Cassius was different from all other males as soon as I met him. It was the first time the *Wild* didn't crouch her shoulders and pin down her ears when a male spoke. He looked so sad standing beside his brother Caleb when he first came down the basement stairs. It was the first time I wanted to ask a question to a male.

Why are you crying behind dry eyes?

He sat beside me on the couch as Belac and Caleb played pool. I couldn't help but drink really fast, the nervous kind of drinking that makes you want to blur the world away. They were strong drinks, more whiskey-vodkas than soda.

He called me Specs.

Cassius's voice sounded hollow, like an old faded echo with the word Specs on repeat in my head.

I started to gag once those whiskey-vodkas dug into my gut. Before I could vomit on the couch, Cassius had me in his arms, carrying me to the bathroom. With the first heave of my stomach, my glasses flew off, breaking on the tile floor. I almost start to sob out loud, but the gentle palm of his hand was running over the ridge-bones of my spine. Soothing.

He held my hair back so I didn't get vomit on the loose strands. My spine was shaking but not from the heaving, from his touch. Deep down I knew right then and there that Cassius could never hurt me in the way I've been hurt. It's not in his nature.

I can hear the laughter from Sunday morning breakfast wisp up the stairs before climbing into the shower to drown out the noise in the rushing water.

Scrubbing, cleaning off the scent of lone sex so none of the wolves at the table can detect the smell in the back of their throats. Once dry, the clothes are thrown in the washer and started.

The stairs are taken with caution, not much noise, only enough to let them know I'm coming down. I hate intruding on them, but Belac left me no choice. I'm staying with the Valentines until she comes back for me. I'm getting used to that and comfortable with the Valentines.

Cassius is at the table with each twin beside him; they are at the end of finishing their breakfast. Rya and Luna Grace are speaking over a table full of baby pictures. The mated wolves send Rya the futures that were created because of her moon gift. Fertility.

Rya is summoned constantly to travel to packs that request her gifts be used on their sterile wolves. In return, the pack has to sign a contract that in a time of need they are to send milk to a pup whose mother has died before the wean.

"Good morning, Treajure," Luna Grace says while I pass her. She places her hand on my head and lets it slide along the back of my hairline. Rya smiles her best smile at me.

"Good morning, Treajure." Rya speaks with the hopes I say something back. I never answer. Never. She doesn't ever give up hope, though.

Cassius's twins have become something more to me than just pups that I watch throughout the day. I press kisses to their heads, and the hum in my throat comes out to vibrate against their skin. I love them.

21

It's been six months since I really understood what that feeling was, but it was right there. Love. Something I never thought would happen again.

Alpha Clinton is sitting in his spot finishing up his coffee, and all I can remember is when Rya giggled to me on her deck as we were watching the waves hit the shore that she thought he looked like a silverback gorilla, and as soon as she told me that, I saw it. I almost laughed out loud. Almost.

When sitting down, I can't help watching Cassius clean both his twins up, wipe their hands, and swat their butts to go play downstairs in the toy room. Chance starts to fuss in the highchair, and Dallas sets him down to play with his cousins.

Caleb stretches out his spine, cracking each bone to the annoyance of everyone around the table. He's drinking milk from a glass, looking out the big window into the backyard. Belac left for the Wilds of Valentine on a Sunday, and I think the both of us should expect her back on a Sunday. So far there's been no sign of her. The Silverback says she's in deep. Caleb argues about going to go get her, and his father argues back that he has to be prepared to make a choice if she doesn't want to come back—will he be willing to live out his life in *Wild* form?

I wanted to argue with the Alpha that I need Belac back, but my voice was blocked by teeth, the sound bouncing off enamel to be swallowed back down deep in my gut. The day she left, my screams were silent for days after. Chin tucked to chest, there was no hope to keep my glasses on. I didn't want to see anything. She left me, and I hated her for it. She told me, promised me she would never leave me. Ever. I believed that promise. She lied. Caleb took the sharpest point of my anger. I stabbed him the way I felt stabbed by Belac. Caleb and I couldn't live together in his house anymore. He felt awkward with me around him all the time. He felt strangled and suffocated. He couldn't take a shit by himself anymore without someone hovering around his space. I paced at night. He got no sleep; neither did I. He brought me to his parents' house and told them he was unable to handle me anymore.

Cassius, in those early days, was the one to sit beside me while I looked out the window. He started to tell me the made-up stories I never knew belonged to me. He has a way of talking to me with a voice that clings to the deeper layers of skin. Not the dead parts that will eventually flake off. He called me a princess, and I thought of him as my prince. My body is made of scars, and in those beginning times, Cassius somehow looked at me without noticing what has been etched into my skin. He actually was looking at me, and he made it so I could never look away from him.

Letter 2

Cash,

The doctor was honest with us. Be honest with yourself. I'm not going to make it. You know it, and I know it. He said not to give up hope, but it's more for you, not me.

I felt the Wild slip away today. I felt her give her last dying bit of energy to the pups, not to me, but for the pups so they have a better chance at living when my time comes. I couldn't tell you this when you asked me about my Wild, if she was all right, because you couldn't feel her anymore. Forgive me for keeping that from you. I wanted you to keep your hope.

She sacrificed herself for them, and I can't believe what I've put my Wild through. I hope to make peace with my Wild in the Moon. I hope she can forgive me. Do you think she can forgive me?

The Wild loved you; she loved you right from the beginning, the moment we inhaled your scent in the clinic. Before our eyes even opened up and saw your face. You were holding my hand, but she thought that it was her paw you were holding. I remember you brushing the hair away from my forehead. It felt like love. It was the second before I opened my mouth and turned your eyes into something that looked like hate.

The Wild never hated you. It was impossible for her to hate you, no matter what you put me through, put us through. I put her through more. She hated me more. She didn't blame you for the hate, the rage, the violence, because it was nothing compared to what she did

24

within me. All those years she had to endure Clayton. All the years his hands were on me she had to suffer under them. She didn't feel his hands the same way I did. She only felt a sickness that came from his touch, not the desire I felt.

Clayton brought me great pleasure, and my Wild suffered because of it.

Every time you touched my skin, she would try to hold onto that feeling, that excitement you gave us deep down. It was her first time to experience those raw primal feelings. She wanted you. No matter how much I spewed at you, she always only wanted you. No one else. She was loyal to you and your Wild, Cash. I need you to know that.

The Wild was your biggest supporter...me, not so much.

There was a time I wished I could sever her from my soul somehow, a way to get rid of her so I could be with Clayton. To be human, maybe? They are the lucky ones; they have a choice. They get to love who they love and not have it dictated to them.

Now that she is gone, really gone, I can't stop the loneliness I feel. I can't stop my suffering inside at losing something that for the longest time I wanted dead.

I've been so selfish. Selfish to the Wild, selfish to you. I never thought love could turn you into something you hated.

Kennedy

CHAPTER 3

Bruises in the Color of an Overripe Peach

Cassius shifts in his seat. His family all notices that he has something important to say. I hold the stillborn breath in. Carson, and Crane, the pussy smasher, hold onto their coffee cups; they have a smell of a hard night of beer seeping from the pores of their skin. They look heavy-lidded and wrinkled up.

Cassius clears his throat—the vein in his neck is pulsing.

He takes a drink of water, pulling in his bottom lip with his teeth. I'd love to feel those teeth on me, pulling my flesh into his mouth.

"Do you want to say something, Cash?" the Alpha asks, and Cassius opens his mouth up, closes it, takes another drink of water. Swallows.

The Luna looks at her male, and Dallas stops everything to look at number three. Caleb cracks his neck before sitting down. Carson and Crane put their cups of coffee down.

Something in the pit of my stomach says this isn't going to be good for me. There is a stutter to the beat of my heart; it's trying to find its normal rhythm.

"I met someone," Cassius tells the entire table on Sunday. The family's special day. The table hears what was told to me last night. I was hoping what he said was just whiskey-drunk lies—that he'd forget in the morning. For a terrible moment, I'm afraid my spine will push through the back of the chair.

The burn in the middle of my chest spreads, growing malignant, unstoppable.

I don't want to burn, not like this. Not this way. The Alpha brings his hand to cover his Luna's. It's hard to watch the squeeze of his fingers. Tight smiles spread around the table. Mine shakes, but that doesn't matter because no one is looking at me. Hope spreads crystal clear on his face with a promise of happiness attached to the smile on his lips.

Blinking.

Blinking back tears because Cassius looks the way the sun does, all shiny and warmth. He's radiating. Biting my inner cheek, forcing an exhale, forcing an inhale. Forcing a smile that shakes raw from the way I'm melting to the bones.

Cassius's head raises, meeting his father's eyes first, then his mother's. He lets them fall on number one, two, four, and five. Rya is next. I wait for my turn. It doesn't come. He doesn't let our eyes meet. I sink in my chair as the glasses fall from my face before I have time to catch them. They land underneath the table, but no one really pays attention to the noise. It's Cassius they are focused on.

Half-blind half tear-filled eyes search for the glasses with fingertips that are stretched out wide, covering as much space as quickly as I can.

"Who is she?" Luna Grace starts to unravel the process of who she is.

"A female that can be claimed. She's one of the females from last night I was introduced to." He says with this calmness that makes my heart bash up against the inside of my chest.

Let the unraveling begin.

"Which one?" Carson asks. His voice isn't strong enough to compete with the blood rushing through my ears.

I sit back up on the chair, not meeting anyone's eyes. I can't look at how happy everyone is.

"Her name's Hazel." There is a surrender of reverence the name brings out from Cassius's mouth. To me, it's a common name. I hope deep down she's ordinary.

"That's a pretty name," Rya says, and I flinch, open-mouthed. No sound comes out, and for once, I am thankful for the silence.

"Hazel is with Tommie's pack." Carson shows why you can always count on him knowing useless things.

"You know where she lives?" Cassius perks up. Everything is now focused on his brother.

"Yes, not far from here. A few hours away." Carson's knee is shaking. I can feel the vibrations through the floor. It competes with my own shake.

"I want an unofficial meeting with her." He speaks calmly, and I have my heart inside my throat with randomness that makes me feel dizzy and sweaty.

"I'll make some phone calls." The Luna straightens out her shoulders.

"I want to meet up with her later today if possible."

The Luna laughs. "No Luna will let that happen. I'll ask, but I think she will make you sit for a while. I'll let you know what she says. Rya, do you want to make the call or do you want me?"

A pause.

"I'll make the call for Cash." Rya smiles through her words to her best friend.

"I could make the call," Cassius casually says.

The Luna and Rya both say, "No," at the same time.

"How serious is this, Cash?" Dallas asks while looking at his hair.

"I want to see her again, unofficially." Cassius rubs at his beard.

"Tell us about her? What was it that made you interested?" his mother asks.

He swallows the pause as his fingers flex away from the fist he was making.

"Her eyes, they caught me off guard."

"Anything else?" His mother pursues more of an answer from her son.

"She's beautiful and looks like Kennedy in a way. She reminds me of Kennedy."

My ass presses harder into the chair.

"Hazel is an asshole, or at least that's what

Tommie says, and Tommie likes everyone," Carson speaks up.

"Why would she be an asshole?" The Luna seems invested in the answer.

"I'm not sure. He just said she was an asshole and likes to take shit that doesn't belong to her. I didn't ask for details." Carson's hand goes over his shaved head; his neck has a red flush to it. I feel like he's sweating out all the beer he had last night.

I feel lighter now. He won't let an asshole around his twins.

"I mean, she's pretty straightforward. Nothing wrong with that." Cassius's voice interrupts the triumph that my heart was feeling for a second.

A bell rings from the playroom in the basement.

"That's my ten o'clock appointment," Caleb announces while looking at his watch. I follow Caleb out of the room because I'm not sure the beat of my heart can take anymore without it failing in my chest.

"Treajure, don't get too close to my ass. I'm still healing from the last time you shanked me." He makes a stabbing motion with his wrist, he gets it wrong, but I don't say anything about that. I hold my spot while he walks down the stairs backward, looking me in the eyes the entire time.

"It was a flesh wound. Stop being dramatic, number two," Crane, the pussy smasher, taunts. He laughs to himself, and Caleb will get him, he always does, but Crane doesn't care. He likes the battles they embark on. One day I really think Crane thinks he can one-up Caleb. I put my faith in Caleb, not Crane. He's too young for the way Caleb can play.

31

A pink child's chair is in the center of the playroom. Caleb is singing at the front desk of Dee's salon. She has everything out to do hair and nails. No red allowed. Caleb had a fit when he saw it was one of the colors she had. He threw a tantrum that even Chance would be envious of.

He yelled into Cassius's face that Dee will not be wearing red until she's twenty-five. Cassius agreed and threw out the color.

Dee looks over the sign-in sheet meticulously. She looks up at Caleb, then back at the sheet, taps the pen to paper.

"Uncle Caleb." She looks around at the pretend crowd, and he raises his hand.

"Please take a seat." Dee instructs him where to sit and proceeds to take his hair out of the bun, letting it fall to his shoulders.

"What are we doing today?" She's got the ends of his hair between her fingers, giving a shake of her head, not liking what she's seeing. Real scissors are in her other hand because her uncle doesn't care if the ends are a little uneven. He makes it work on him.

"I was thinking a trim, and I need my nails done." He looks at his bare nails; the polish already has worn off. She grabs a hand, inspects each nail, then the other one.

"You're a mess." He agrees with her.

She snips and snips, too much from the right, not enough from the left, but to her, it's a masterpiece that her uncle praises. Nails are next, a light pink that bleeds into the skin surrounding his cuticles. She takes her time, he is patient, and before long

32

he's all done and it's my turn.

"Perfect." Her voice is excited. She is getting better and better with each appointment.

"That will be twenty dollars." She holds out her hand, and Caleb puts a fake twenty in it with tip. I've signed in as well, and Dee looks over her list before calling my name, "Specs."

The rest of the morning is spent in the salon, while Chance and Ken play with their toys. They refuse to sit for hair or nails.

Our games switch from salon to school to making a spaceship out of the box the new fridge came in. We draw windows and buttons on the inside so we can blast off into space after we eat our lunch inside it.

One by one they each lay down, sleepy-eyed, before I curl up beside them at the entrance. Afternoon naps at their best.

When I come out from the cardboard box, Cassius is sitting on the bottom step. I'm not sure how long he's been there. He closes his sketchbook and holds it in his hand. His hair is pulled into a bun, and he's taken a shower and trimmed his beard. He's got on a few shirts that stretch slightly across his chest. Clean jeans, not joggers. He even is wearing socks. He's still wearing his layers, but something is different. I notice immediately.

"I'm going out this afternoon." His words bubble up like champagne in a flute on New Year's Eve when everyone cheers to a better New Year. I never thought while raising my glass this year that this would be his year.

Raising my head quickly, I push the glasses up

the bridge of my nose.

"Uncle Caleb is taking all of you to his house." The way Cassius talks, this makes me feel included. *I'm not his child.*

The pups squeal. Before racing up the stairs, he grabs each one of them, nudging his cheek against theirs.

"I'll be back tonight," he affirms when he turns to walk up the stairs. I get the view of material shifting with the way the muscles on his back flex and relax.

Rya and Dallas are there, along with Carson. Cara and Cottom are also standing at the door. Cottom presses himself against the wall as Caleb goes by; he looks the same way he looked the first time Caleb entered Belac's house. He held the scent of Belac's spread legs on his mouth, and she held Cottom's smell down her throat. Wary, alert, ready to run really fast because Caleb's claws were out and so were all his teeth before Belac had to get hers out to channel Caleb away from Cottom's neck.

If I close my eyes, I can still hear Belac telling Caleb how he ruined her life when they first met. That everything she has built is for nothing because it's expected for her to be marked and taken away by him. The hatred I heard from her was always reserved for her brother, never anyone else. It's the first time I ever saw her cry. Caleb had no idea what to do when she started crying. He opened up his arms, and Belac told him to go away, for now. She cried all night long; I was the one to hold her for the very first time. I held her until she fell asleep. She woke up assigned to her fate, shoulders bent, not the leader she was the day before. When her brother told her what was going to happen she spit in his face, and they fought. It's not the first fight I witnessed between them, but I felt as if it would be their very last.

"I wanted to do this myself." Cassius's voice pulls me out of those memories.

"We want to come, plus Cara and Cottom didn't go to the party last night. The Luna was excited for all of us to come as soon as possible. She has a beta that has been rejected by his mate, and her son lost his mate a few years ago. There are two available females there as well." Rya points all the reasons that all of them should go, and Cassius relents with a nod of his head.

"I'm ready. Are you guys?" Dallas is letting the pups go out the front door first with their suitcases on wheels. Caleb nudges the shoulder of Cottom before going out the door. Cottom does not move. Not even blink. He lets the male go by him. Never provoke Caleb.

Cottom found out the hard way when he tried to joke about the situation between them. Caleb wasn't laughing. He's no jester.

Caleb destroyed Cottom's face. Dallas had to pull him off the male who couldn't get off the ground after the altercation. Currently, they are trying to find Cottom a new pack to go to. Clayton's pack seems like the perfect fit, but Caleb visits that pack a lot.

Cottom doesn't want to leave until Belac comes back, but I'm afraid for him if he stays. The violence is escalating. He wants to say his goodbyes to our leader of the Wildflower gang, as Rya likes to call her. To her, we are *Wildflowers*.

Everyone makes it outside; Caleb is holding onto Dee's hand while trying to keep the two small males out of the front ditch. He turns toward me. "Aren't you coming?" I shake my head no and open up the passenger side door to Cassius's truck.

"You're coming?" Cassius frowns.

I nod my head, looking straight ahead while clicking my seatbelt.

"You shouldn't come, Specs." His hand squeezes into a fist. I want to ask him why, but the armor of my teeth keeps everything inside; nothing is able to escape through the small gaps between enamel.

The drive is quiet. He doesn't talk over the radio like he always does when it's him and me inside of here.

I watch the way his fingers grip the steering wheel, flexing his hands at times. He actually checks his face in the mirror, and I want to tell him he's beautiful. The words stick like thick syrup in my throat. It's hard to swallow.

Letter 3

Cash,

Dallas is back without Rya and I can't help but feel relief for Clayton.

I hope Clayton is happy. I hope Rya can forgive him. After all, she forgave me in her own way, didn't she?

36

I would be lying if I said I wasn't jealous. I am. I am so jealous it's hard to breathe. I hate her most of the time. I hate her so much my gut hurts. When I found out Rya was Clayton's mate, I wasn't that jealous of her. She wasn't anything I should be jealous of and Clayton didn't really seem affected too much by the bond.

We were cruel to her, we were cruel, and looking back, cruelty isn't what love should be.

My jealousy grew over the years, as she grew. We didn't see her a lot, but when we did, I would watch Clayton and see if he was affected by her. Sometimes I would catch him staring at her. I'd catch how more and more his eyes couldn't look away from her. Then she went away and I prayed she'd stay away.

Every time Clayton tried to mark me, my hatred for Rya grew. The mark never stayed, and after some time, it hurt to be bitten by him. It hurt so bad that I had to tell him he couldn't try to mark me because I couldn't take the pain from his bite. When your teeth sunk into my neck, I thought I actually could die from pleasure; it was so intense that I came. You felt me come with your teeth dug deep. Your mark stayed and I fucking hated

37

you for it, but deep down, I wanted you to do it again and again so I could pretend it was Clayton that was doing it to me.

I hated Rya when my heat came. Clayton couldn't get me pregnant. We would pray to the Moon together to give us a miracle at first, then we would curse the Moon for her selfishness. Clayton and I could have made a beautiful family.

I'm looking down at my belly right now, watching the twins move inside me, and sometimes I pretend they are Clayton's, and you are just a dream, a terrible dream.

You thought things would change when I became pregnant, that I'd come around. The look on your face when you found out I tried to get rid of them. All I ever wanted was to be a mother, and here I was trying my best to kill what was inside me. You took the silver hook from my hand and I honestly thought you would put it through my throat. I begged you to do it.

I knew that changed you. I knew seeing me with my legs spread and the blood on my hands that it changed you. If I ever hoped of being loved by you, it vanished that day. I don't blame you for everything that happened after that. I blame myself more.

The way you screamed at me, it shook my wall I built to combat you, the bond, everything. Your finger pointed at me and you yelled, that all I wanted for the longest time was to be a mother. Then I screamed back, that you were right, I wanted to be a mother but not to your pup. I told you that the pup would come out weak just like you. I told you I could never love something so weak and small. I told you that you could never measure up to Clayton. You let me slap you that day. You let me hit you over and over again until I fell down. I think I bit you, and you didn't hit me back, you went quiet, and I think that was the scariest I ever saw you. Something inside you broke that day. I felt the snap.

You shaved your head, and I wanted to die.

That scene always plays out in my mind. If you didn't come at that time, I think I would have succeeded in killing them. I don't think I would have ever been able to forgive myself if I did that.

I apologize for saying all those terrible things to you. They won't be weak because they came from you. I was angry. Anger drives you to say things you don't mean. Not an excuse. I shouldn't be excused for what I have said to you. I just want you to know I'm

39

sorry.

Sometimes I think my love made me become this monster willing to kill anything that stood in my love's way—even my own children.

I'm sick. I feel sick that I could even go there, to try and kill my pups because they came from you and not him.

When you read this letter, burn it. Never let the twins see this because it would fuck their minds up if they knew their mother wanted to kill them. They would be fucked up for the rest of their lives if they knew I tried to get rid of them. Tell them their mother always wanted them and that I love them.

Kennedy

CHAPTER 4

Peach Bruises Form after the Study in Scarlet

It feels as if I've started to bleed internally when the truck stops.

"Are you all right, Specs?" The palm of his hand cups the back of my head to trail fingers down my neck to rest on my shoulder. I feel the weight of it. Heavy, warm, tender.

I want to say, "Look at me, I'm right here," but I can't say it because he's staring right at me.

He frowns, clearing his throat.

"Have a drink of water." He twists off the cap, handing me the bottle. It's hard to drink, even harder to swallow. I choke, and he rubs my back in small circles with his fingertips.

"Don't be nervous; I'm right here. Nothing is going to hurt you in there. Nothing. The evil queen can't get you when you have your knight by your side." He brings his made-up fairytale story between us as he searches my face. Cassius gives me a crooked smile, and I have no choice but to follow his lead and give him mine back.

It ends with him getting out of the truck and me closing my door. I follow behind him, watching the nerves knot along his spine. Even his breathing is changed, and he wipes his hands on his jeans. He never gets nervous. Never.

It starts with me pressing the flat part of my palm between the shoulder blades of his back, trying to ease the tension. He leans his spine into the touch. I wasn't prepared for that.

"Thanks, Specs." The smile he gives me curves at the edge of his mouth, and I want to curve myself sideways just watching that face.

Dallas's knock on the door draws the smile away from Cassius. Rya is holding a jar of honey that she gives as gifts to the packs she visits. They are from the wildflower garden she planted in a barren spot that was hard to grow anything in the territory. Now it's full of life and the best honey is made from it. The farm even makes wildflower soap now.

Cassius takes a long breath and fixes his face straight.

"Welcome, please come in." The Luna of the pack is there to greet us all with a smile showing a hint of teeth.

"I brought a small gift for you, and thank you for letting us come today on such short notice." Rya hands the dark honey to the Luna, who is smiling wider. A very respectful smile, I think that's what Luna Grace would say about it.

"It's wildflower honey. My mate has several beehives on our territory that she takes care of in her spare time." Dallas's voice is light when his eyes fall on Rya's.

"You've grown since the last time I saw you. How's your mother and father doing?" The Alpha isn't bigger than Dallas, who now is exactly the same height as his father. Luna Grace made a comment a few months ago about noticing how Dallas is coming into himself. She squeezed the Silverback's hand while pressing a kiss to his eye that was swelled shut. It was the first time Dallas got the best of his father.

"Good. They wanted to come, but Cash thought it best they stay home. This isn't official."

"Understandable. This is my son, Tate." A male steps forward with his hand outstretched.

"Dallas." His hand engulfs the other male's hand.

"This is my mate, Rya." Dallas holds Rya by the hip.

"My brothers, Cash and Carson."

A hand reaches behind, pulling me from my hiding spot.

"This is our Treajure." Dallas has a way of making me feel that I belong to everything.

A gasp from the Luna with her hand over her mouth. Pushing my glasses back up, I keep my head raised. I feel like peeing.

"Is she from your pack?" The words are bristled out.

"She's part of our pack now." Rya's tone is in direct contrast with the Alpha's tone.

"What pack did she come from?" Every pack I come into contact with wants to know where I come from. They hold hunt in their voices; they just don't understand that the man is a hunter and nothing survives long once he catches you. They all would die, and I would be the cause of it if I open my mouth and talk.

"We don't know where she comes from. She doesn't talk much." Rya presses her chest into my back and gives me a soft hug from behind. A nudge of her cheek to mine.

"It's nice to have you here, Treajure. Please feel at home in our house." The Luna steps closer; I have to concentrate not to pee when she presses her cheek to mine. Rya is holding my hand, and I squeeze hers back.

"This is Cottom, and this is Cara." Dallas finishes our informal introductions. Cara tries to look at the future Alpha, and he doesn't give her any notice.

We are directed toward a table that can't even compare to the Valentines' table. Nothing can compare to that table, ever.

Dallas sits directly across at the end of the table from the Alpha. A place of honor. Rya takes his right. We all sit down after that. Cassius keeps looking around because there are no females here. Maybe she decided not to show up and I could almost sing. Almost.

There is another male wolf that wasn't introduced by the Luna. He's a big wolf, just as big as Caleb, not much smaller than their future Alpha, Tate. He keeps looking at Carson.

A hard knock on the door before it's swung open has Cassius straightening in the chair. The ridge of my spine stiffens because two she-wolves walk in who make my shoulders sink down.

No scars, no glasses. "I brought the wine." No problems speaking even if she sounds nervous. I don't understand why she's nervous; I'd love to be what she is.

"What a treat for us." The Luna takes the box from her hands.

"This is Addie and Hazel." There is pride held in how the Luna says *Addie*. I thought for sure she would be Hazel. The way the Luna says *Hazel* is filled with distaste; she can't even pretend to smile through the name.

Caramel would be jealous of the color of her eyes, with a hint of mint that clings around her pupils. They remind me of Kennedy's picture that Cassius tells his day to in the middle of the night. She's fully female, fully on display, and fully stoned out of her mind. Lips open, then half-close. She has great hair, I think to myself while touching my own hair.

This is what bleeding feels like, watching him look at her. He's never looked at another female that way before except for the wall picture and on very rare occasions I thought he looked at me that way before he turned his eyes away to focus on something else.

He is soaking in the rays of her while I can't help feel the wilt of skin and bones.

Blood rushes in. "This is my mate, Rya." He sounds far away introducing everyone.

"This is Cottom, Treajure, and Cara." I have to tear away from his eyes to look into hers that grow wide, then half-lid back down. Hazel sways with a

45

wobble. She might be drunk too.

"My brothers Carson and Cash." There is a tug of a smile on Cassius's lip; my heart bleeds for that smile. I'm bleeding out in front of everyone, and no one even knows.

"I thought this was an unofficial visit?" There is something sharp and stabbing behind Hazel's words. She points a slender finger at the son of the Alpha. Her face is all fire, and a vein in her forehead pulses.

Cassius stands. "They insisted on coming. If it were up to me, I'd be alone with you right now."

I am bleeding…

The words blaze a fire through me. I'm burning up—turning to ash by what he just said. I don't want to burn, not this way. Not like this.

"Really." It's sneered out, through teeth that flash, sharp and white. She's no longer soft; she's stone-edged. Her focus seems to come back as she sits down. Disgruntled.

"Would anyone like some wine?" The Luna seems nervous. Hazel has a fight in her eyes when she regards Cassius.

Hazel reaches for a bottle of wine, fills her glass to the rim, leans over, and loudly slurps from the edge. She smiles now. I look at everyone and everyone is watching her like she's a show you can't look away from.

Her fingers curl around the stem of the glass, knuckles blanched white.

Without any manners, she lifts the glass to her lips and pours the wine down her throat in one swallow. Even Crane, the pussy smasher, would be

46

put to shame with how fast she just chugged a glass of wine back.

She pours another.

There is a belligerent look in her eyes toward Cassius, with a lifted lip flashing whites in disrespect. If I had a knife, I would throat cut her.

Carson is open-mouthed, Rya shifts in her seat, and Cassius looks unbothered.

"Addie, this is good. You made this yourself?" the male that wasn't introduced says, loud and proud. Impressed.

"Yes, it's my grandmother's recipe, but I made it." Her face blushes, lips unloosen, a smile creeps out.

"What kind of wine is this?" Rya is focused on the wine, not on Hazel, who is taking bigger and bigger swallows from her glass.

"Honeydew wine. It's made with the leftover fruit I have in my garden. I have honeydew, apple, and pear wine." Addie's shoulders seem to curl around themselves after she's done speaking. All eyes are on her as she stares at her plate.

"It's delicious," Hazel slurs, exaggerating the word delicious. Her second glass of wine is gone and she's moving on to the third.

"So, Tommie, what are you doing now?" Carson asks the male who the Luna never bothered to tell us his name. Tommie, it suits him.

"I'm working in the investment division in the pack." Tommie shifts in his seat. The tips of his ears are red, with hair falling into his eyes before he pushes it back.

"Really? I thought you were being recruited hard

by that firm in the city." Carson leans into the table. I can't stop staring at Cassius, who can't look away from Hazel.

"I decided not to go with them, not a good fit." Tommie sips on his drink; he swallows loudly.

"Did you go to the same school as Tommie?" a female asks that is sitting beside the Luna, who just asked Carson the question.

"We went to school, even had a few classes together. We did some training as well." Tommie's hand goes through his hair. His neck is red.

Hazel gives Cassius eyes that could maim. She doesn't like Cassius, and for a selfish moment, I want to scream thank you to the Moon.

"You look familiar. Have we met?" Rya asks Tommie, but all I can hear is the pounding of my own heart, because I can see the pound of Cassius's neck vein, dilated and pulsing.

"It could have been at our house. He was there once." Carson now shifts in his seat, and Tommie takes another sip of wine.

"You went to their territory with him?" Tate, the alpha's son, speaks faster than my pulse.

"What's that supposed to mean—*with* him?" Cassius's tone claws around the table.

"Nothing, I'm just surprised, that's all. I never knew he had friends outside the pack," Tate explains, and it makes it sound as if he thought Tommie was a loner.

"Did you ever have your head shaved?" Rya still pursues the fact she's seen Tommie before.

"Yes, I shaved it all off once." Tommie's shoulders straighten out; it makes his shirt tighten across his chest.

"Why did you shave your head?" Hazel's tongue seems thick in her mouth. The words are mashed together.

"It tells their pack females I was available to them. The males shave their heads, and it says they are available, but when they find their mate, then they let their hair grow out. Not available. The females wear red showing that they are willing to entertain a male." Tommie tries to explain this to Hazel, who gives a cold stare toward Cassius.

"You shave your heads if you're available?" Hazel speaks directly into Cassius's hair.

"We do." Cassius gives a stern voice back.

"Then why isn't your head shaved?" Her voice is saturated in the wine she's just consumed.

"Because I'm not available yet."

"Then why all of this if you aren't available?" Hazel looks at everyone in the most disrespectful way. Why isn't the Luna taking her to the backyard?

"I'm here because of your eyes," Cassius speaks—I cringe. Hazel finishes the glass of wine.

"So my eyes brought you here, not me?"

"Yes." Cassius's honesty makes me feel as if today won't have me burning up into ash.

"What a waste of my time." Hazel's eyes molest into his.

"This was a mistake. I apologize for taking up your time and my family's time. Obviously, you aren't who I thought you could be." Cassius stands and walks out of the house.

My bleeding has stopped.

"That's all right, I'll send you my bill in the mail, because unlike you, my time means something." She sways in her seat.

Tommie stands. His hand digs deep into his pocket.

"Here, I'll cover his bill. I expect change back, because your time really doesn't have much value now, does it? Look at you. You really have no respect for yourself."

Everyone pauses.

Mouths come back together after a few seconds.

"He's just mad I stole his stuff. Don't pay him any attention. His thong is riding up his ass." Hazel reaches for the five-dollar bill, shoves it down her pocket.

"I won't be giving him any change because I'm worth the whole five." She stands, gives a few sideways steps, takes a bottle of wine for each hand, bows to us with a smile as sharp as a scalpel's edge, and leaves.

I jump toward the big window to watch that wolf. She is drinking right out of the bottle, and when she passes by Cassius, she gives him the middle finger to his face, and a big fuck you.

"Treajure, it's time to go." A hand to my shoulder and Rya ushers me toward the door.

The engine idles even after all the other cars have pulled away.

We sit together quietly before he pulls out of the driveway.

Hazel is on the side of the road with a crooked walk. Bottle to lips.

"I want to take another look at her."

The truck rolls by her slow. A muted, slurring taunt from her mouth that has this smile on Cassius's mouth.

The window rolls down. "Fuck you," Hazel says before placing the bottle back to her mouth.

Cassius has to feel that; I felt it. It's full of pain, rage. It's biting down to the bone. Her words don't hide behind a wall of teeth.

She speaks to leave bruises.

I feel that fire rise again with the way his bottom lip forces the curl of his top lip up. My lips are forced own, hard. The flame is too much; the scorch is too great. I'm burning—bleeding.

I don't want to burn—I've bled enough.

Letter 4

Cash,

With Clayton, the beginning was easy; he was always there. We slept together early, too early for some. Our parents knew what we were doing and didn't care. They were so sure we were mates, that when I moved into his room, no one questioned it.

When our parents found out we weren't mates, they demanded I go to my own room. Clayton fought them on that. He fought and fought and fought for me, for us. He promised me that he would love me forever, and I promised him I'd love him forever.

I have to apologize for what I said to you

51

about my tattoo when you fucked me that day. Clayton doesn't own my pussy, but neither do you. I put his name there so he understood how much I loved him and wanted to be with him. I knew that when I met my mate, I would reject him, just like Clayton rejected Rya. I wanted to show him that I was serious about us, just like he was serious about us when he got my name tattooed across his back.

You really stood no chance, Cash. None.

I'm sorry for laughing in your face. I didn't know that was your first time doing anything with a female. What I did was cruel to you. You're not defective, you're not disgusting, you're not repulsive. You're perfect, and I should have told you that instead of writing it now in this letter.

Everything is right about you, from your hands to your lips to your cock. I'm sorry I was cruel. My love for Clayton brought out the cruelty in me that I never thought I had inside me.

I was lying when I told you that you couldn't satisfy me the way Clayton could. I lied to you when I said I couldn't even feel it inside me. I lied. I could feel every thrust, every pump, and it makes me wet just thinking about how good your cock felt inside me. I lied to you that I was faking it when you called me a liar that I couldn't get off from you. Not once did I have to fake anything with you.

Also, you're not a shit kisser. I lied about that too. Sometimes I want to kiss you so bad, but it was never the right time. I thought you would kiss me again. You never tried again after I laughed in your face and told you everything there was wrong with your mouth, your tongue. Your mouth is perfect, and your tongue is something that I have dreamt about at night. I wake up wet from those dreams. I haven't had a dream about Clayton in a long time. I've been dreaming, fantasizing about you and what could have been if I wasn't such a bitch to you and you weren't such an asshole to me.

Clayton was always kind to me. He put me first. He was gentle and caring; he included me in every aspect of his life.

With you, I wasn't treated kindly. You weren't gentle or caring, but neither was I, right? You didn't include me in anything.

You took everything away from me, and I made sure you understood that you were nothing to me. I'm sorry, Cash.

Kennedy

CHAPTER 5

Scarlet in the Color of Blood

Tension is held into the deep muscles of Cassius's back. No matter how much he tries to roll his shoulders out, it remains dug in.

He's not smiling.

I'm trying to figure out how to tell him that Hazel's not the one.

His face seems marbled. Difficult to read, but not feel.

He's a deep bruise in the color of an overripe peach. Fading soft tones that are replacing the darker ones. There is a want at times to shout out, *"Bruises are good, you can heal from bruise—they are only a discoloration of flesh, not mutilated skin. You'll heal, Cassius. You will heal."* The words get stuck behind the armor of teeth that leave no space for anything to slip out of the cracks.

"Do you think that was a mistake, Specs?" He's watching the road, not me.

I say nothing.

Cassius clenches the steering wheel with a tight jaw. Molars pressed.

He swallows.

"I saw her, and she reminded me of Kennedy." A barely heard voice over the crunch of tires on asphalt. In the cab of the truck, it's a shelter, away from his family, away from the twins. I can see him through the lenses of my glasses. He's perfectly seen in the shifting streetlights that we pass by. A shudder runs between the blades of my shoulders, perfectly straight down, honestly felt.

We drive. He turns on the radio, and low music fills the space inside here.

The leather cushions the back of my spine as I get comfortable to listen to him. He talks more to himself, if I am honest. I wish it was to me, not some confession out loud to be heard by no one. Sometimes I wonder if he thinks I'm no one?

"She's mouthy…violent." The edges of his eyes get smaller, reminding me when he's about to smile. He does. I want to add, *"She wouldn't be a good fit with the twins. Mouthy and violent don't mix with precious and vulnerable."* My mouth remains shut, but my mind is screaming, loud and clear.

Torment eats away that newly formed smile; he frowns instead. "What am I doing, Specs?" His hand drops to the side. The edge of his baby finger could touch my thigh. So close—it's unnerving.

"I should apologize to her. It was a mistake to go there. She's not Kennedy. I was lying to myself. I saw her eyes and thought she could be Kennedy. I was wrong. Really wrong." He grips the wheel. Tight.

"Do you think I was a dick?" Now he looks at me, and I nod yes. I want to shake my head no, but I'm no liar.

"I've got to do something." The streetlights brush his shadow away momentarily before casting his side profile back into the early night. Hidden and dark, until the neon light comes again, flashing his profile in brilliance and awe.

I shift in the seat, thighs pressed together.

"I've got to change. I can't live like this anymore. It's not good." The music is playing, and I've noticed he hasn't turned off the songs like he usually does when it's just him and me in the truck. It's like he can't stand to finish what's playing on the radio. He doesn't really enjoy the sound of music like most wolves do.

Alone like this, the flame is starting underneath my skin. Warmth turning to heat.

"Can we go for a drive?" Cassius licks the dry cushion of his bottom lip. I try not to lean closer to him.

No answer from me, he must feel it means yes.

The truck turns on the highway heading in the opposite direction of his territory. I know where we are going.

This is his self-destruction...

I've been on this route several times before. All those times left scars to both of them. Real flesh wounds that tore through the bruises that have been left against their skin, gouged deep to the bone. Kennedy's death has left Cassius and Clayton bone-scarred.

Hard lines with sharpening eyes start on Cassius

57

the closer that we get to Kennedy's birth pack, reminding me of the very first time we came here together.

The first time the Alpha had to come and get Cassius from Clayton, he told his son that nothing was here but ghosts that couldn't be seen. Cassius screamed back, *She's not a ghost.* He told his father that he wished he could see her one last time to make things right. *One last time,* he cried into the Alpha's chest when he was dragged away. It was his crying wish.

He smelled of salt clinging to his wet cheeks all the way home that night.

"I'd give anything to have her back to say goodbye. I didn't get to say goodbye." Despair pushes out from a mouth that tightens into a punishing line. I want to tell him we have no magic to make wishes come true. We can hope, pray, but wishes are only wishes from the needy.

Right now—he is needy.

The shadows are starting to paint him haunted; the light lets me see his need.

He blinks harder, trying to watch the road the closer we get to Clayton's territory. Another long blink crushing the lids of his eyes downward. Nothing leaks out.

We take the back way in; his breathing has changed. So does mine.

This isn't good. This never has a good outcome for either of them with Cassius showing up at random times of the night.

We come to a halt in front of Kennedy's old home. Only waist-height weeds remain. The engine shuts off.

Behind his lids, there is movement from eyes that aren't seeing the outside, but the inside of his mind.

What does he see in those memories? Will they be the color of mint like the sweet story he told me of how Kennedy was an artist? Her favorite medium was working with charcoal. Her fingers would be stained in black and would smudge everything she touched. That story trailed off, sweet green turned into a jealous green in the same breath. He then told me, she liked to smudge him, draw pictures on his body with her fingertips. He hit the wheel hard; a bruise bloomed on the meat of his closed fist. It was purple, black, but faded fast to the color of an overripe peach. Then the color turned to rose petals and started to blaze. Solid, deep red when he got out of his truck, slamming the door and screaming for Clayton to come to him.

He wanted his turn. He was promised his turn. He was promised a turn. He's been in line long enough.

Clayton showed up, spitting sparks himself. This was their moment. No one to stop the grown males from destroying themselves. Not each other. *Themselves.*

Two males for the same female—fighting. Except the female is a memory, a ghost. Neither gets her if they win the fight. When Cassius decided to fight with teeth, Clayton told him, "I fight with fists only. I can't kill you, even though I want to. I respect your father and Dallas too much. Caleb is my best friend. My only friend. I'm not ruining that.

We can fight with fists whenever you need to, but never teeth, Cash. Never. Teeth."

Cassius spit blood, screaming, "I want your throat." Clayton stood there facing Cassius.

"You can't have my throat, only fists, Cash." Clayton called the Alpha to pick up his son. The wait was long. I peed my pants. Not once but twice.

Violence is my trigger.

It wasn't them that I saw fighting or their blood scented on the breeze. It was silver sliding against my skin, my blood in my nose and down my throat. It was them that I heard. Heavy breathing the closer they got. Slipping, falling, tripping over and over against. Crawling to get away. *Running.*

Shadows were changing shape. Someone was behind me; I was sure of it. Shapes became the bodies of men. The scent of urine in my nose, laughter. The hiss of pain was my own. Sound was dangerous, but I didn't learn that until much later with my captures.

I didn't understand that he loved the sound of pain, misery. He loved the sound I made at the height of when pain almost took over completely, right before the body folds upon itself and shuts down.

He thought if he could make memories of pain that I would stop trying to run. I never stopped trying. I never stopped when he thought I was dead. They were upset with him as he put me in a plastic garbage bag; they left me for dead at the dump. The sound of Clayton's voice was what brought me out of that memory. He kept speaking to me until I looked at him.

"You, female. I won't hurt him. Calm down. You're Treajure, right? I was told about you." It was the first time Clayton spoke to me. I couldn't answer him because the smell of urine and plastic was everywhere. I could taste the smell of that memory. I made a sound deep in my throat, and Cassius stopped fighting with Clayton.

I was frozen.

Nothing wanted to move on my body. Not even my head or my hands to pick up my glasses that dropped at my piss-stained feet. Clayton had to handle Cassius for hours before his father came. The Alpha stormed into the territory loud enough for my bladder to release itself again. He picked me up, and I climbed his body, trying to press myself underneath the Silverback's neck.

"Specs, are you all right?" The voice of Cassius shuffles those memories away.

Blinking.

I'm sitting in a dark truck with him, looking at waist-high weeds where a house used to stand not long ago.

His hand is on my thigh, a rub, a squeeze of flesh from the pad of his fingers. I wish his fingers would leave some kind of mark on my skin. He's too gentle. Always so gentle with me. I think he's afraid to hurt me. I could never be hurt by his touch.

"You smell afraid." I turn my head toward his voice.

Shaking. Not from fright.

He's gotten close.

His hand raises—I flinch.

Chaos when his skin touches mine. The pad of

his thumb drags down my cheek, to press against the skin of my neck where my pulse feels thready and weak.

"Tell me what's wrong, Treajure?" There is a lowness to his voice that makes my desires drive forward. He's started to use this sound on me, and it makes my knees shake, and my belly grows hot.

Opening my mouth, forming the words, I can't shove the sound out. The effort of speech goes against everything I've been self-taught.

Shaking hard—but trying even harder. I want to talk. I want him to hear me.

No sound...

He leans in. I get closer to him.

A finger traces my mouth that still is open.

"Why are you scared right now? Don't you know whatever you're scared about has to get through me first? They can't get through me. Not the evil queen, not her warriors. Nothing can get through your knight, Treajure." For a fragment of a second, I think he might kiss me. Here, now. In this truck.

I lean in, closer. He doesn't pull away.

"*See me*," I scream in my head, "*see me*."

The windows have fogged up. It's getting hot in here.

"You don't have to be afraid anymore, Specs." My chin is gently held in his hand. The edge of his thumb draws small circles on the line of my jaw.

Closing my eyes, I feel unbalanced.

"Don't be nervous. I'm here with you." His calm sways my body.

A kiss is placed to my forehead, staying longer than a brush of skin. When he pulls away, my face follows his lips.

"That evil queen did a number on you, and if I ever get a chance to find who did that to you, I'll hunt them, Treajure. I will hunt them and show them the same they have shown you. I promise you that. If there is a chance at finding them, I will get them." He's toned in destructive violence, the *Wild* in him flexing outward in a show of teeth. His *Wild* has been showing himself to me more and more. He's even made a few attempts to nip at my skin before Cassius pulls the teeth away with a shake of his head.

Cassius doesn't understand; the man would hunt him with silver and turn him into something caged and terrified. His body would be used for the man's sick pleasure.

"Specs, you've come a long way, but I think you can go further. We could go further." The heat of his hand sinks into my thigh. It's all I can think about. The weight of him on me.

"We need to change, Specs." He's serious. So am I when I nod my head yes.

"I need to do something. I can't live like this anymore." Grief-stricken, Cassius takes a hard breath in. I can feel his voice, every inflection of sound skimming over my skin. He's full of pain, full of misery, *full of need*.

"I have to change something." The palm of my hand rests against the beat of his heart. I want to dig myself in there.

"We could change together. We could go further, together." Words are spoken raw and truthful by him to me.

He's all scorching fire, and I'm going to be the leftover ash. I know it. I can feel it. I'm afraid to be blown away from him. Please, don't let me be blown away with his change.

Letter 5

Cash,

By now you already know these aren't some undying love letters to you. Knowing you, I think you thought they would be, but knowing me now, you understand these aren't going to be words that you pine over in the dark.

I've lost myself. I don't really know who I am anymore. Who am I?

With Clayton it was easy. I was his as much as he was mine from my earliest memories, but with you, I'm your mate, but am I really yours? I honestly don't think so. You're upset reading this, I know. Sorry.

The look on your face last night was something I wasn't prepared for, but I didn't ever plan to have you ask me that question either. Why ask me things that are better left under our rug? I guess our rug can't cover everything. Our pile has grown too big.

I'm sorry for wanting to kill Rya. It was like a baton struck me across the face and all

I could taste was my own blood trickling down my throat because I knew this was not the same juvenile that left the pack. Rya was an adult wolf who had grown into her position. Luna. I fucking knew it as soon as I saw her in the office that day collecting the keys to the midwife's house. I knew it, and I was terrified to have Clayton see her again. How do I compete with her? How? His mother couldn't wipe that smile off her face. I was standing right in front of her and she couldn't hide how happy she was that Rya was back.

She told me things were going to change. I just never knew how much. I had this growing fantasy that if I could kill Rya, then everything would go back to how it was really supposed to be. Clayton would be able to mark me and we would become a family as long as when I met my mate, he'd do the same thing. Kill him.

You asked me last night if I would have been happy if you died. I told you yes. Sorry, that hurt you. It hurt you a lot. I could see it all over your face. I thought you would be sick when you sat down on the chair. After a few minutes of not saying a word, you told me you were going to bed. I slipped in beside you later that night when I knew you would be asleep. You weren't asleep, but you pretended to be. I know when you are really sleeping and when you're not.

I was so jealous of Rya when she came back that all I thought about was killing her. How could I compete with her? I didn't think a wolf could be that beautiful. The way she looked, her hair...but her eyes. Her fucking eyes were the blessing from the Moon herself. How could I compete with a wolf who was given the Moon's blessing? I thought killing her would give me everything I wanted. How does love turn you into a monster? I justified it to myself. Killing her, killing you, would let Clayton and me be together forever. So I thought. I felt Clayton slipping further from me. I felt it; I knew it a little before Rya came back. But when she came back, I knew we were slipping further apart. It was a matter of time, and I couldn't let go of him. I couldn't even imagine my life without him in it.

Clayton and I were lying in bed the night she came home. I was curled into his body, and I asked him if he thought Rya was beautiful. He didn't answer me for a few minutes. I knew deep down before he said a word that I was in trouble. He didn't lie to me;

he found her very attractive. He said she was a beautiful wolf, but it wasn't her that he loved, it was me. That night we made love, slow love, the kind that you remember long after it's over—it felt like goodbye.

You and I have never made love, and I'm afraid we never will now.

I asked you a few days ago what you thought of me, if you thought I was pretty. You told me I was the prettiest thing you ever saw. Ever. Then you opened your mouth back up and also told me looks are deceiving, and on the inside, I had an ugliness that made you turn into your own ugliness.

I'm afraid to look in the mirror anymore. I don't want to see what's inside of me. I fear it.

I see you, Cash. I see the inside of you, and I think there is an ugliness, and underneath that, there is a beauty that I never allowed myself to see.

Kennedy

CHAPTER 6

Blood can Drip from Words

Naked and bare, his open eyes look directly into mine.

"Why do I always find myself here?" The past de-focuses the pierce of his blue eyes. It's never out of his head. Never. We almost always end up here, sitting in front of this house that isn't standing anymore. Sometimes he tries to push the tears away; other times he lets the tears push out.

"I can see her. If I close my eyes, I can see it all."

A pause. "She loved that house. Even to the end, she loved that house." Raw words from a tightening voice.

"Kennedy loved him right to the end. Deep down, she couldn't stop loving Clayton, and here I am unable to stop coming back to him." He exhales. "I have to stop this." My reply is unspeakable behind a wall of teeth.

"How do I stop?" A rebellious tear wants to

squeeze from the side of my eye. I fight the need to cry for him. He doesn't need my tears. He needs someone to listen to him when he decides to talk about Kennedy, about letting her go, so he can let himself go.

"You have this way of seeing through me. You see right through me. Like now, like the first night I met you. You had this look on your face that you knew exactly who I was. It scared the crap out of me. Did you know that?" I shake my head no.

He sighs, and I try not to squirm, because he's now scratching blunt nails down the skin of my thigh.

"Sometimes I feel like I could tell you anything, and I want you to know you can tell me anything, too. I won't judge you, like you never judge me, no matter how bad I get." He looks at me as if reading every single facial feature I have.

"I wish I knew what you were thinking. There's more to you than this. I know it." When he says these kinds of things, it makes me feel that someone understands me; it makes me feel free to look around at the world or look at him. It's hard to look at males, but Cassius has this way of making things easy to look at. Like the time he took me to my first barbecue at Caleb's place. Belac left, and I just started to sleep under Cassius's bed. I didn't want to go. I hate crowds and the noise. I didn't want to pee my pants again in front of people. It's embarrassing even though no one makes a big deal about it. It's a big deal to me. He let me scrunch his shirt in my hands the entire time. We sat there, and he talked to me the entire time about really nothing, but he talked and I listened. He didn't like talking to the wolves, either. He gave them some grunts and short answers, but he didn't want to socialize just as much as me. He was there for the kids, not himself, and he told me if he had to go, then I had to go too. We could suffer together. Soon I looked forward to going to parties with him. It meant we sat close together and he would be free to talk to me about anything he wanted to. Most times it was the kids or asking if I liked the shirt he got me; he can never buy himself something new without getting something for the kids or now me something. He's been buying all my clothes now. Caleb said he could do it, but Cassius told him *no*. On rare occasions he'd look at the dance floor and look at me, and I thought he'd ask me to dance. He never has, but recently he picked up Dee and had his first dance with his daughter in front of the pack, and Luna Grace cried while Caleb took a picture.

Ten minutes go by with the only noise coming from our lungs. He's breathing through his nose, rough with haste.

"Change with me, Treajure." Cassius's voice is the only thing that disturbs the air inside the vehicle.

I'm holding my breath.

My hand is studied in his. He turns it this way and that, tracing a deeply scarred line that split the skin when it was made.

My wrist bone spindles underneath his touch, twisting in all the ways he moves my hand.

How do I change if my pieces aren't broken, they're missing? Lost. Buried treasure somewhere that even with a map it would be hard to find.

CASSIUS

Our palms press with fingers outstretched. I compare the size before he weaves our fingers together.

"You have small hands," he says as if noticing this for the first time. The pad of his index finger rubs at the webbing between my thumb and finger.

Every muscle in my body contracts. When everything unusually relaxes, I can't stop the "hmmm" that comes out from somewhere deep.

"Do that again. Make that sound from here." His breath lingers where the sound came out of. The edge of his thumb is pressed against my voice box, sliding up and down on the thin skin.

Arousal pits deep. Vision blurs.

It's hard to focus on anything else besides him, his voice, his low breathing. I want to reach out, tug at his hair, feel the coarseness of his beard on my face. I want to rub myself against him. I want him to feel me.

I want to feel the rub of him.

A slow finger runs along the inside of my arm, and his nose touches the shell of my ear, skimming against the ruby earring.

"Do it again, Treajure." His voice pitches even lower. His hand on my thigh doesn't pull away. The weight of his warm palm soaks into the material of my pants.

A brazen shiver runs loose—without balance. The sensation is overloading.

"Hmmm." The sound is said with eyes closed and thighs pressed together.

"I know you can talk, Specs. I know it."

Opening my eyes, it's impossible to move. He's

71

staring right into me.

I watch his lips as he pulls on an edge with peaked teeth. He might kiss me. I wait. He doesn't.

"I need to change, Specs. I'm no good this way. I'm no good to anyone this way." He shifts away from the space that I feel is my refuge.

A knock on the window is startling. Cassius's emotions sluff off his face to be fixed with a blankness.

"Do I need to call Caleb, or will your father be needed?" The window isn't rolled down, but we can hear Clayton clearly.

"You won't have to call anyone," Cassius says as he opens the door and steps out with shoulder attitude.

"Are you sure about that, Cash?" Clayton's voice seems purposely controlled. Subdued even.

"I'm sure. I was just looking at the house." There is nothing there when Cassius turns his head in the direction of the tall weeds.

Clayton scratches the side of his jaw with the edge of his thumbnail. He's clean-shaven with a shaved head. It's very rare that he makes the first move; it's always Cassius.

"I have a question for you." Cassius's words are teeth bared. There is a subtle alert in the stiffening muscles on the side of Clayton's neck. I watch from the backside of the truck, using the metal to block my body from two males who will fight, because there are thick things between them, *like blood*.

"What's the question?"

"All the time you two were together, and look at you. All clean and shaved." Cassius continues with teeth bared, words meant to bite into bones.

Clayton's strides are efficient, confident, not vain.

Both of them seem to loom at the other. Their fight never seems to bleed out; there is always more blood to be spilled.

"What do you mean by that?" Clayton asks.

Cassius crowds into Clayton's space.

"Let's see," Cassius says, "all the time with Kennedy and you can move on. You make it look simple. Easy even."

There is a feeling of a trigger being pulled right before the explosion of sound.

Clayton fists both hands into Cassius's shirt, pulling him close. Eye to eye.

Teeth bared, breathing flared.

"I haven't moved fucking on." Clayton's words shake from his mouth, and spit flies from between clenched teeth.

"I'm not fucking over her." Clayton struggles on his words; he sounds like an old wound reopening again. Words leak out like blood.

A torn second holds between them.

Clayton uncurls his fists from Cassius's shirt.

"I have obligations. My sister needs me. My nephew needs me. The pack, whatever is left, needs me. Not a day goes by that I don't think about everything. Not one day goes by that I don't think about her. So don't stand there and tell me things you know nothing about," he snarls.

Clayton is still mostly an open flesh wound, stuffed with his own self-made tragedy.

"You took everything away from me.

Everything." Cassius's blood drips now in words that come out like a split-open gut.

"No. You took everything from yourself." Clayton points his finger in Cassius's face. It's met with a hard fist from Cassius.

Both of their bodies collide as their war spreads and tramples down the weeds underneath their bodies.

Blood and snarls mix.

"You were the one who let her die. Don't blame me for what you did to her." Clayton's words hurtle the pain across Cassius's face. The sad part is that Cassius accepts that as his truth; meeting him was her death.

"I loved her, and I thought she would be safe with you. I was wrong. That's why I let her go with you. I thought you could be something to her." Words strangle, blanching both their skins.

This is more a warring of blood-soaked words than scraped knuckles.

"You tore out her throat. How was that safe?"

"I didn't do that. The *Wild* did. I would never hurt Kennedy. Ever." There's this feeling of a sputtering matchstick newly lit, the violence growing as the flame takes hold of wood.

"I let her go. I couldn't give her the one thing she truly wanted in life: pups. You could give her that. You. Not me. I knew that when I was put on the pole, and I wanted to die knowing that she would get everything she wanted with you. Instead, she died." The violent flame between them catches, burning brighter.

"You have two kids that you need to raise, and

you're here? What kind of fucking father are you? She would hate this. Raise the kids she always wanted to have." That is savagery at its best, because it brings out the long teeth from Cassius.

"I'm raising my kids."

"Are you? How, when you're here with me? Grow up, Cash. Be a father. See what's in front of you."

Flesh lacerates, and I stumble backward.

Triggers flash, glasses slide off. The world becomes hazed. The taste of blood coats the back of my throat, and I'm hurtled back into memories that have no place in my mind.

The feeling of claws scratching over my gut, except it's not claws, it's silver-tipped nails that he uses to scratches lines into my skin. He pushes fingers into my mouth and calls me a *fucking miracle* as I lay on top of the bed, healing. I try to dig, splitting nails into his skin, as the taste of iron washes down, bloating my stomach. I'm mitted with a silver collar around my throat. I'm afraid that the oxygen will rot in my lungs before I'm allowed to take another breath.

This is terror.

Can terror be both noun and verb? Can it?

"Treajure." The afterimage of him is still pressed behind lids even when I open them up. His shadow seems to remain even when I'm looking into the blurred face of Cassius.

I have to blink a few times. Once isn't enough to get rid of the shadows. My glasses are put back on my face, and Cassius's bruised blues look down into mine.

"Let's get you home." I'm in the sanctuary of strong arms that feel like safety and the word *forever*.

"It's not fair you drag her here with you. Look what this does to her. Look at her."

Cassius says nothing back.

"You're fucking selfish, Cash. All you can think about is yourself. That's what killed her, you being selfish. You haven't changed. I've been waiting for you to grow up and stop acting like you're the only one who lost someone. You aren't, but I give you all these excuses, and so does your family. It's time, Cash, to stop making an excuse out of yourself." Clayton is in his face, and Cassius is holding onto me with a grip I've never felt before. It's as if he needs me to hold on to and not the other way around.

"At least show Treajure some respect and stop bringing her here. She shouldn't be here. You know it, yet you still bring her as some kind of excuse to yourself."

Cassius's head hangs low. His shoulders have curved in as he puts me into the passenger seat.

"I'm sorry, Treajure." There is a breach of emotion in his words. He can't look at me.

The door shuts gently, and when we drive away, it's the first time that Cassius leaves on his own and not dragged away with blood still clinging to the undersides of his nails seeking more violence.

Letter 6

I wrote letters to Clayton. Please give them

to him. I know it will be hard for you, but please do this for me. He has a chance with Rya, to be happy, to have a family that I couldn't give him.

Don't read these letters. Don't read them. They aren't for you and you'd only be hurt more.

I want my chance to say the goodbyes we didn't get to have.

A proper goodbye.

Kennedy

CHAPTER 7

Words Felt in Velvet

The tread of tires on asphalt is all that's heard for the longest time within the truck.

The sound reminds me of the way his truck would pull into the warehouse, almost silent except for the grind of tires. He was meticulous with the hunts, a new location every time. Never the same men. Never. Two men waited by the doors, excitement noted in their dilated eyes. Rich men, powerful men waiting for me. Crossbows in gloved hands—not silver-tipped, injuries will heal. I have to make it look believable that they killed me. That they were the hunters and I was the prey. My mother, father, brother, mate all killed by his loss of control. He waited out my shift then it was my turn to be stalked, to run, to try and escape, but "never too hard," he would say. Don't try so hard. I can still feel the scream against my skin because it was always met with the lash of silver. The stinging bite that he would purposely not go too deep, but he'd eventually lose his temper and those times I was left on the top of the bed, bleeding into the mattress, waiting to see if I would heal. I always did, but barely. I was this bleeding girl spread out like a crime scene for these men of particular taste to fawn over with congratulations on their good kill. Some would come alone; others would come in pairs or threes. It was different every time. What wasn't different is him with an open duffle bag counting bills with a smile spread like cold ash across his face. A silver bracelet on my wrist to prevent my *Wild* from teaching him, them who was a hunter and who was prey in those early days when I thought I could win. They had no idea what I was, but he knew what I was. He knew it all, his *fucking miracle*.

"Sorry, Specs." His voice slides my eyes away from the window to look at him. Memories of old bones and blood fade.

He frowns. "You've been through a lot, and I'm putting you through more. I'm selfish. It feels better not being by myself on the drive home." His hand reaches out, tightening the knot up in my throat.

His hand on wrist, my skin explodes in the sudden sensation.

"I can feel your heartbeat. What's going on in that head of yours?"

I can't say a word; my teeth won't allow it because of a knotted-up throat. Difficult to let even a swallow down. My glasses fall off the bridge of my nose, and I don't put them back on, not right away. I like the blurry. I like the feeling of my wrist held in the palm of his hand. The weight of him, gentle and caring. A shiver shuffles between spinal bones. This is enough, I think. This is more than enough for now. Him holding me. It's enough. For now.

"Were you thinking about the evil queen?"

Drilling my top molars into the bottoms, I give him a nod, yes.

"You know she can't get you, right?"

I don't nod my head yes. I keep still and silent, but the throb of my heart is in my ears because of the wrist grip. Desire devours in the feel of his skin on mine.

"One day you're going to need to tell me what happened. Not today. One day."

There is nothing to say back to him. Not a no, not a yes. Nothing. What could he do with the secrets I would tell him? Nothing.

The side of his thumb draws circles around my wrist bone, over and over again, reminding me of the way he first got me away from the window on a Sunday waiting for Belac to come back to me. He gripped my wrist, thumb drawing circles, and his steady voice gave me the first story of the evil queen. He talked for an hour, I listened. The *Wild* within turned her head and observed this male beside her. She angled her ear to mouth, not listening, more noting the infliction of his voice, the rise and fall of sound that brushed her fur down and calmed the stiffness of her curled down tail. She relaxed around him, and so did I in that hour of storytelling. After that, we paid more attention to Cassius. We followed him and settled around his space. The stories kept coming, and before long, I thought of his space as my space. This would be enough, I thought. For now, that was enough being in his space, but something began to happen between my thighs, something that felt tingly and alive—full of unrelieved pressure.

His breath is felt pressing along my inner wrist; he's brought my hand to his mouth. He sniffs. I'm still not wearing the glasses, and it feels nice having the road blur by and his breathing is all that I can focus on.

"It gets ahead of me. You make me scared, sometimes." He releases my wrist with a broken breath out, picks up my glasses, and hands them back to me. I can hear the hard grip of the steering wheel.

I want to ask him how could I make him scared? He's never once made me scared, not once. Never.

The light on the clock says it's 12:45 a.m. It feels earlier than that, more a ten o'clock feel than after midnight.

"I shouldn't put you through that."

A stretch of self-inflicted silence as he seems to be chewing on unsaid words.

"He was right about the twins. He has a point." I can hear the grind of his words. Some words can feel soft and kind, while others can be textured rough and abrasive.

"I shouldn't waste my time with him. I should be spending it with them." He takes a big breath in, filling his lungs as his words fill the space inside the truck.

"He was right about a lot of things, Specs. A lot of things he was right about." He's not looking at me; he's focused on the road ahead of him. He puts his turn signal on, and we move to the next lane.

"I have to come back here once more, and after that, I'm done. I'm fucking done with all this." Anger and sorrow weave and spread across his face.

Everything is dark when we enter the house, and Cassius goes straight to the picture of Kennedy. He stares at her unchanging face while I stare at him, and everything else is forgotten.

One picture that has him tied to the past to keep the present distant.

He's not at ease within the world.

"I need to change, Specs. I'm no good like this. Not to anyone." I get to watch his reflection leave the glass of the picture.

He's half undressed by the time I make it into our room—pants are being tugged down thighs. His socks are off before I have time to close the door. The layers of shirts are nothing but a crumpled pile by the bed. Sometimes I think I see the *Wild* move within him. The dark creates this delusion that has a possessive feel and lingers long after he's crawled into bed, laying on his back over the top of the covers, his eyes facing the ceiling. I'm not ready to go to bed, not yet, not with the low light resting along his hip bones. How would it feel to climb up on his bed? I'd like to feel the soft bulge in his boxers harden. How would it feel to curl into his side and nudge my nose into the hollow of his neck, inhaling until I fell asleep?

I undress fast, picking up one of his worn shirts, slipping it over my body—it's still warm.

He turns his head to the side, catching the

Moon's glow outlined within his eyes. He's watching me standing in the middle of the room, watching him. His eyes roam from my feet to land heavy on my chest. I can feel my nipples through the shirt.

He looks back up at the ceiling. "You need to wear more to bed, Specs. You're too big to wear my shirts now." He crosses his arms over his chest and turns his head once again to face me.

"Did you want something, Treajure?" His low voice doesn't interrupt the deep night. I watch the way his throat moves with a swallow.

My mouth opens up, but nothing comes out.

He breathes out through his nose, long and controlled, and I have lost my breath.

"Goodnight, Specs." He turns over with his back facing me and his face to the wall.

I'd like to slip past boundaries and reach out, touch him... Instead, I stare, and this is enough for now. It's enough for now, I think as I slip underneath the bed with my palms pressed against the baseboards, trying to feel for the movement of his body above me.

This is self-destruction. To love him is to love ruin. Can ruin ever love you back?

Letter 7

Cash,

You wanted to talk last night. I just couldn't talk about that. Not Kimberly. It's a subject I couldn't talk to you about.

You wanted to know how could I? How could I have done that to someone I loved or thought of as a little sister?

At the time, I justified my actions and said a baby would bring the family closer together. I'd watch the baby when Kimberly went to school. The baby would make things between Clayton and me better. His parents would have something to think about other than getting me away from their son. Clayton's mother would see how good I was again. We would bond over the baby.

It wasn't some plot having Kimberly become pregnant; it just happened. That day, her mother asked me to bring her a plate of food to the secure area. I saw Jake sniffing around, nosing into any cracks he thought he could see. He was pawing at the windows, and I smelled the scent he was spraying along the side of the container.

Kimberly and I talked a long time, and I felt bad for her; it's something all females have to bear, the cold sweats, the pain, the cramping, the unrelenting pressure inside your cunt to be smashed into so you can burst open. Kimberly was sweating and holding her stomach. She was in real pain. I know that kind of pain. It's what drove me to you.

When I was going to lock the door back up, I stood there looking at the key in my hand, and I had that first thought. If Kimberly had a baby, everything would be better. The family would get closer; the heat would be off Clayton and me. Everyone would be concentrating on her and the pup. I wanted that baby, too. I wanted a baby for myself. It all came like flashes, the way I could raise the pup because Kimberly was really young, and she still has high school to finish then college. It would be years before she would be independent enough to move out with her mate, who was still at school. I'd convince the family and Jake that he needed to go back to college so he could support her. I needed Jake out of the way for the now-budding plan to work.

The more I thought about things with that key in my hand, the more I saw this future that could be mine. I wanted that baby, and when I walked away from the secure area, I didn't lock the door.

You asked me how could I love Kimberly like a sister and do that to her? Simple, I loved Clayton more than his sister, and I would do anything for us. That's how I justified it in my mind. I was building a future for me and

Clayton, his sister could have more pups, ones that are hers, but this one would be mine. Sacrifices are made for love, and this was a sacrifice that would be made.

This is easier to say writing it on paper instead of talking to you and watching your face. You have a hard time hiding your emotions, and that disgust would spread across your face and I'd see it, and maybe I'm selfish, but I didn't want to see it, so that's why I told you I couldn't talk about what I did to Kimberly.

Jake and Kimberly only needed one night, because when her mother went to her in the morning, she found them still locked up. She had to pour cold water on him to get them apart. She asked me if I locked up last night, and I said yes; it was the very first lie I ever told her. I told her yes, and she looked at me. I'm not sure she believed me, probably not. I prayed to the Moon that it would be enough, their night together. I prayed and prayed, and when her heat was done and she didn't bleed, I cried with her, not because I was scared like her, but because I saw this as a new beginning. A new start. A baby!

We had a family meeting that included Jake and his mother. I made the argument that he should go back to college, he needs the education to support her and the babies, or else he's going to be working some low-paying job for the rest of his life. I knew that would dig into your mother. She hated the thought of her daughter living a lesser life than the one she has now. Her Kimberly was never without anything, she had the best of the best, and now she was looking at Jake, who was just an average male with an average future, and that female couldn't stand that. So I drove in on the fact he needed to leave to better himself and that would better them in the long run.

I needed Jake gone so Kimberly would have me. She needed only me.

I honestly thought it would work out, I thought it would all work out in my mind and we would be this happy family once again, but Rya came back and everything fell apart.

The world isn't fair, I thought. The world isn't fair.

Kennedy

CHAPTER 8

Velvet Made Memories

Cassius is still sleeping when I come out of my space. I must have fallen asleep before him.

He's curled up with his face to the wall, as if to protect himself in sleep.

Caleb's at the spine of the house eating breakfast. I love how Luna Grace calls the table the spine of the home. He hesitates for a small moment before spooning more cereal into his mouth. He chews louder—I'm annoyed.

"Why are you looking at me that way?"

I roll my eyes, and for some reason that gets underneath his skin, and I try hard not to smile.

Heating up some hot water in the microwave, I have to drink this mixture the healer gave to me every morning to prevent my heat from coming again and again. When I reach for the carton of milk in the fridge, it's empty. I look at Caleb.

"Sorry, used the last of the milk." My smile stops from curling while his spreads wide and deliberate.

"No pouting, Treajure. You're making me feel bad. You know I love you like a sister. But we know you don't love me like a brother, because no sister will shank a brother in the ass again and again. I have real scars."

Dallas calls them flesh wounds, but Caleb acts like he's dying from a little blood. He shoves another spoonful into his mouth, chews louder.

"Have I told you that I like your earrings? I do. They suit you." I stop making the tea to recover from his words. I can feel the rev of my heart rate. I don't look at him.

"Those are pretty rubies, really pretty noticeable rubies." I pour the hot water over the loose-leaf herbs, spilling some of the water that I have to wipe up on the counter.

"They suit you. Good choice, Treajure." The words beam out from the curve of his mouth.

He leans into the table. "You should wear your hair up more often. That way no one can miss how pretty they are." The air conditioner isn't on, but I just got a cold chill.

"When do you think Belac will come back?" He's stopped chewing, waiting. I could tell him she'll be back on a Sunday. Belac is a wolf of habit; he doesn't know that yet. He will. I could answer all of the nonstop questions about her he has. He cornered me only once, asking what's her favorite color, her favorite type of music, food? He wouldn't let me out of his space, and that was the second time I poked him with my silver switchblade. In the fleshiest part of his ass. It went in smooth so that, at first, he didn't even feel it. That's how sharp I made it.

He demanded the switchblade be taken away from me; there are kids around here. I kept the point angled to his throat while his mother told him the only child here was him and that he was the one that made me go there. I felt threatened, and she understood I had no choice but to give him a little shove back from my space. He pointed to his ass and asked if that looked like a little shove. Shoves don't bleed.

"Treajure, focus, I asked you a question. Do you think Belac will be back soon?"

I rap my nails on the cup, taking a moment to inhale the herbs, before giving him a shrug of a shoulder.

"What's she like, Treajure?" He keeps the distance between us, the spine of the house separating our bodies.

I'd like to tell him she's the warm lap you can always depend on. She's kind and loves beyond what's normal. She makes anyone who meets her feel important and that they belong around her. She doesn't like cocky wolves like him. In fact, she loathes that trait in any wolf. It reminds her of her brother, and I've never known a wolf could hate so much. Family brings the worst out in Belac. The worst.

Caleb points his empty spoon at me. "Not going to answer?" He makes it a question that I don't answer.

"My dad told me this morning that Belac split the wild pack. She became a leader wolf, taking the runts with her. They are headed up north." His spoon drops in his empty bowl that holds the excess of milk in it.

"She didn't like how the *Wilds w*ere treated, so she took them away." He smiles, and I can't stop thinking how clueless he really is. I want to scream, *she's a leader wolf. A. Leader. Wolf.* Clapping my hands between each word for emphasis that he can grip onto.

"Did she love that wolf?" Caleb can never say Cottom's name; he calls him *that wolf* or *him*.

He looks in pain, and blood floods my mouth from biting back words that could make him feel better. I do shake my head no, and I can see the relief stretch across his face. To Belac, it was fucking, nothing more, something to keep her arms full at night, instead of how empty I know she always felt. Family means a lot to her, and her family was the hollow left in her chest after the fucking. I'd hear them on top of her bed; she even asked if I wanted to join her one night. I couldn't; I wanted to let them know I've never done that before. My flesh might be ruined, but I did keep something special for me to keep safe. He took everything from me, and I think he would have taken my virginity if he liked females. I would have to watch my mate be raped by him, over and over again on top of the bed. He would pray to the Moon at night not to heal from him, not to stop the blood, but he always healed until the next time.

He died after being used too roughly with silver. The man always wanted to push the limits of our ability to heal, he went overboard one night and

Oaken didn't stop bleeding, and we talked that night until he couldn't talk anymore. He made me promise to try and escape, he made me promise if I did escape to find someone who could protect me. He made me promise to try and forget about this when I escaped, and every chance I got, I tried to escape. But he was too fast for me before I shifted. He always caught me. When I shifted, he blew silver dust in my eyes to hobble me. I was never faster than him after that, and sometimes I would lose hope that I would never fulfill the promise I made to Oaken.

"Treajure, you're sweating." Caleb's blurred; my glasses have fallen off.

"Where are the twins?" Cassius's voice is right behind me. He's got his hand now on my shoulder. A small squeeze before going into the fridge and closing it.

"Mom has Dee. They went out for breakfast and a girl's day. Dad and Dallas have Ken and Chance. I guess there's been some kind of bee massacre, and Rya has them looking for the killers." Caleb puts his bowl in the sink and washes it before drying and putting it away.

"Hornets maybe?"

"I don't know. I didn't want to get involved in their hunt. I just got my nails done. Dee would drag me if I ruined her work." He checks out his nails with a small curl of his top lip.

The back door opens, and Crane, in yesterday's clothes, strolls in, stretching his back with this lopsided smile on his face.

"Where were you?" Caleb asks.

"Out." Crane smells of stale beer and lots of sex.

"You know you shouldn't be out at all hours of the night, doing who knows what."

Crane gives Caleb a side-eye but says nothing. He drinks a glass of water.

"Stop sounding like Dallas." He scratches at the side of his hip, lifts up his shirt, and he has teeth marks there that are fading along his side. Multiple teeth marks.

Caleb looks at Crane with disgust written across his face.

"What are you looking at? I'm not doing anything you haven't done. Well, I do it better than you," Crane taunts. Caleb huffs through his nose.

"You should be spending time with your nephews and niece. They're only young once."

"I spend enough time with them. Remember, I'm their favorite. Uncle Crane is their favorite uncle." Crane can instantly get underneath Caleb's skin.

"Is that what they tell you? They lie. I'm their favorite, hands down." Caleb and Crane constantly fight about this, trying to outdo the other.

"The both of you are getting played by three-year-olds."

Both of the males look at Cassius as if he's said something so off the wall that it's the most ridiculous thing he's ever said.

"I heard your meet and greet didn't go as planned." Caleb's words make Cassius's shoulders stiffen.

"Not how I thought it would go. I'm going to go there and apologize to her." Jealousy punches at the lower part of my gut. Why does he have to see the female again?

"You have a problem seeing what's in front of you, Cash."

"What do you mean?" Cassius squints slightly; he looks confused.

"You'll figure it out." Caleb's eyes flash to mine, and he looks away. I feel the heat cling to my earlobes, and I want to crawl underneath the table. Caleb knows. I might get sick. If he knows, then everyone will know, because he can't keep any kind of secret. He likes to tell everyone everything.

"You think Hazel's sober?" Crane laughs. How did he find out?

"I would think so." Cassius goes to the back door and grabs his keys.

"Let me drive. I have to mail a few pictures. I got this new printer paper, high gloss, the colors pop." Caleb's up and out the back door.

I can hear the music already thumping inside the van. When he bought the minivan, everyone laughed at him. He got it custom painted, matte black, big rims, limo tint windows. He told his parents he's a family wolf now, but it doesn't mean he can't have style. He also told everyone not to be jealous and don't copy him. They all need to come up with their own ideas.

Cassius opens the side door up. Once inside, he closes it behind me.

"Juice box?" Caleb reaches under his seat and pulls out a few boxes.

Cassius shakes his head no, and so do I.

"I fucking love these." He spikes the box and sucks it up in one gulp, collapsing the container from the inside.

Once he's done a quick two, we are on our way toward a she-wolf who doesn't understand how lucky she is.

Letter 8

Sometimes I think love can be a disease or an addiction, or at least for me it is. My love grew and grew until I turned into something malignant that ate everything in the path of my love. I'm not sure there's a cure for me. I'm not sure how I can be cured of my love for Clayton.

The thought of Clayton and Rya together keeps me up at night. I'm happy Dallas came back without Rya, but at the same time, I'm fucking struggling. I want Clayton to be happy. I want that, but a selfish part of me wants him to not be as happy as he was with me. Fucked up, right?

Do you think they're fucking by now? I can't stop thinking that Clayton is fucking Rya. It bugs me so much that he is probably fucking her. I wonder if he's marked her yet? Is she better than me? I hope not. I know every line of Clayton. I know him better than he knew himself, and he knew me. He knew everything that I liked or didn't like. We had no idea what we were doing when we were young, no idea. We learned together; we learned everything together. We hid it at first. We would sneak away to our island, the place where you found me. That was our secret spot. No one looked for us there. Ever.

It started off innocent at first, you show me yours I show you mine. But once you get a taste for that, there is no stopping wanting to do more than look. We started to touch each other; we kissed. Terrible at first, but we got better and better at it. I watched him the first time he was able to come, I was there for that, and he was there for mine when that happened to me with his fingers buried deep into my pussy and a finger in my ass. I came for the first time on his lap with my legs spread and his teeth pressed against my neck in our secret spot.

It was only natural for things to lead up to him and me having sex. It was once again clumsy, he couldn't get it in the first time, but we kept trying until we both were left with blood smears between our legs.

He told me he loved me as he cleaned me up, and I told him I loved him, too. It was magical, on our island with only him and me. We always went back to our island; we went there to be alone, to live in our own world. We were our love story there in the cushion of moss. In my young mind, he was going to be my mate, and in his mind, I already was his mate. We just needed to shift to make it official.

Our parents knew. Our parents didn't stop us. After all, our parents told us there was a good chance we would be mates. Everyone was excited when Clayton started his juvenile transition. I had this big plan on how we would announce it at school, and I'd be wearing this amazing outfit. I even had the nail polish picked out and what my hair would look like. I honestly thought I would be the next Luna, and everyone else thought so, too.

I want to be the best thing that ever happened to Clayton. I want him to be happy, but fuck, I want him to think back and realize I was the best. He loved me the most, and no one could love him better than me. I am so selfish. I am so fucking selfish that I want to be the one Clayton can never get over. I want him to realize that not even Rya can be better than what I was to him.

When you think back on me, I want you to know there is better out there than me. I want

97

you to know that I wasn't the best thing for you. I want you to understand that I really was never yours. Find yourself someone who loves you, that love the twins as their own. You will have a chance now to be loved and to give love back. Don't fuck things up because you're destroyed by my death. I destroyed you way before I died.

The world isn't fair, Cash. It isn't.

Kennedy

CHAPTER 9

Memories that Start Out Bitter

Caleb turns the wheel and looks at his brother, says nothing.

Silence crawls between them. A few minutes pass by, and I can feel Caleb has a lot to say; he's just not talking yet.

"Clayton called me last night."

"Yeah." Cassius says the word sharp, clear and on edge. That's the edge between these two brothers, Clayton.

"He said that you left on your own."

"Yeah." Cassius looks out the window, not at his brother.

"It's a start." Caleb doesn't look at his brother. Hopefully, time stops being stagnant now for Cassius.

"I guess it is." He's still looking out the window that's slightly rolled down. His jaw muscles clench and unclench.

"Clayton's looking for a Beta, Cash."

"That's not even funny. Stop."

"Not interested?" Caleb mocks surprise.

"What about you? You're his best friend." The edge of Cassius's tone sharpens.

"Still hostile?"

"Always." The word seems to break between the *l* and *w*.

"You need to work on that. You can't go through life hostile. Wolves notice, kids notice." What Caleb says makes the side of Cassius's jaw bulge out for a moment before relaxing. I used to think that Cassius was hostile, but I found out that he's shy, and a little hostile, but shyer.

"Dallas should have killed Clayton." It's not the first time I've heard Cassius say this. Probably won't be the last, either.

"You know why he didn't, right?"

"I don't care why. He had an opportunity and didn't take it." His words feel grizzled and chewed on.

Caleb touches his forehead, looks in the mirror, before those eyes hold on mine.

"If Dallas killed Clayton, Rya wouldn't be left with a choice, and eventually she would have hated Dallas for taking the choice away from her." Caleb talks patient and slow.

"Still, he should have killed him." Betrayal to Cassius is lethal. It eats him from the inside.

"Then what? He's dead, then what?" Caleb's calm, but I can feel the tension roll off Cassius.

"I guess he would be dead, and that would be it."

"Would it be it? Would it make that much of a difference?"

100

"To me it would. Maybe not to you, but to me."

Silence bunches in a tight fist on Cassius. Caleb is tension-free, loose with his hair blowing in the wind because he rolled down the window all the way.

"Clayton thought it was a big step for you."

"Fuck Clayton. Fuck his big step." Cassius is riled up now with a hostile point of teeth.

"You can tell Clayton I'm only seeing him one more time, and that will be it. No more."

"Listen, Cash, I'm not your go-between. You have something to tell him, tell him. Don't use me as some sort of message machine bitch." Caleb reaches down between the seat and pulls another juice box out and crushes it in a swallow.

"Why one last time?" He's curious now, leaning slightly toward Cassius.

"I have something to give him, then it's over between us." Cassius looks out the window.

"I could give it to him if you want?"

Cassius's head turns quick, his mouth opening slightly. "Are you for real?"

"What?" Caleb asks, and Cassius shakes his head with his tongue held except for the directions turn left or right.

"You seem mad. Are you?" Caleb pokes.

"I'm not mad."

"You seem mad. Are you?" More pokes and Cassius grinds his teeth.

"We should do dinner tonight, my house, homemade pizza grilled on the barbecue. The kids can make their own. They like that, and maybe you can bring your better mood with you, Mr. Moody."

He pokes some more, and Cassius starts to laugh under his breath after a while.

"This road, turn here." We drive slow. Cassius is scanning the area.

"Pull up here, beside the black truck." The back of a male is facing us, and it looks like he's locked out of his truck. He keeps trying the handle before he hits the side with the flat palm of his hand.

Cassius rolls down the window all the way, and the wolf looks at Caleb and Cassius before nosing inside. He stops, holding his eyes against my face. I'm polite; I smile, shoving my glasses back up the bridge of my nose.

"Tommie, right?" Cassius is not good with names, but he remembers this wolf's name.

Tommie pauses. "Cash, right?"

"Right, this is my brother, Caleb." Caleb gives him a nod, Tommie's eyes fall all over him, and for a minute Caleb seems uncomfortable with the attention.

"I was wondering if you could tell me where Hazel lives?"

"Why?" The look that comes across Tommie's face is very telling. Hazel is not his favorite wolf. I think it hurts him to say her name. It comes out sounding like rubble grinding together.

"I just wanted to apologize to her for yesterday. Clearly, I made her uncomfortable." Tommie laughs with his hands on his knees, bent over. He laughs and laughs with tears starting in his eyes. He holds his gut.

"No, you didn't. She doesn't rattle easily. She's not here, anyway. She's left for Vegas on business."

My heart jumps in triumph. Not here. I try not to smile. I try.

"Do you have a number I can call her at?"

Tommie's grin seems murderous as he reaches into his back pocket.

"As a matter of fact, I do." He hands the card to Cassius, who touches the picture of her eyes on it. Caleb takes the picture from his hands and grunts with a disgusted shake of his head before tossing the picture back at his chest.

"Tommie." A female on a bike rolls up with a small pup on the front of the handlebars of her bike and a male maybe six riding the pegs on the back frame.

She parks the bike before coming over to the truck. She has those delicate pretty looks, with a small nose and nice lips. Her eyes outstate her face, big and welcoming.

"Hello, Cash, hi, Treajure." She remembers our names. I give her a little wave.

"Hi." Cassius, by his tone, has forgotten her name. Addie's eyes fall to her feet. If she was wearing glasses, they would have slipped off her face.

"Addie, her name's Addie. You just met her last night." Tommie's words come out aggressive. Caleb straightens himself out. I can see a hint of teeth between the crack of his lips. Maybe even a small rumble from his chest that has no effect on Tommie.

"I knew that." Cassius voices over the rise coming from Caleb's *Wild*.

"What are you doing here?" Tommie ignores

Cassius, turning to Addie. She lights up. Caleb's back fur rises, and Cassius is calm.

"I brought them for a swim. They get crazy if they are cooped up in the house for too long." Both the pups are off and running toward the backyard.

"Gotta go. Nice seeing you again. Cash and Treajure." Addie waves to us before turning and following the running pups.

"Cash, you should call Hazel. Tell her I gave you the card. Make sure she doesn't charge you the full price, not worth it. Trust me. She likes to be haggled with." Tommie once again has murder spread across his face in the form of a smile.

Caleb pulls out of the driveway before opening his mouth.

"Not sure I like that wolf," Caleb announces.

"Why?" Cassius asks.

"Did you see how he was looking at me? He either wanted to fight me or fuck me." Caleb sounds a little shaken.

"Are you afraid to fight him?"

"Fuck no, I could take him. It's just he looked at me a little too long. I felt like meat." Caleb turns the wheel quickly, and I feel myself leaning to the side.

"Carson and Tommie went to school together."

"I knew it, he wants me."

"Not everyone wants you, Caleb."

"You're right, not everyone, but most do." Caleb turns up his smile.

"I don't think Tommie likes Hazel."

"What gave you that impression?" There is a flatness to Cassius's voice.

"Did you hear how he said her name? It was like

his skin was being carved up."

"True." Cassius scratches at his beard.

"So Hazel. She has pretty eyes." Caleb picks up the card again, looks at it, throws it back at Cassius's chest. I want to scream, *Toss it out the window, we don't need it. You don't need her.*

"She does have pretty eyes." A ghost of a smile traces on the words that just came out of Cassius's soft lips.

"With a card like that, I wonder what she does in Vegas?" Caleb taps at the steering wheel with the palms of his fingers, nails pristine, not a chip in the paint. Cassius frowns.

"Are you really going to call her?"

"Yep."

Caleb regards me in the rearview mirror before his eyes slide away.

My turn to look out the window and think quietly that I have to stop these feelings toward someone who will only leave ash in his wake.

Letter 9

You called me damaged, I called you insane. I'm not damaged. I was never abused, I was never hit, and I was never raped. I didn't grow up with hunger; I didn't grow up with parents who fought or had problems. I'm not damaged. My fault is I can't get over love. I can't get over Clayton. That's not damage, that's heartbreak.

But you, Cash, I've ruined you, haven't I?

This isn't some kind of heartbreak for you, because you have to be in love for heartbreak to happen. Let's face facts. We don't have the love. We have the bond. We have that between us but not love. You're dealing with ruin, and I'm dealing with heartbreak.

It's going to be hard, but you're going to need to try and stuff your self-pity somewhere else after these twins are born. You won't be good for them if you can't rebuild what I destroyed. You need to be good for yourself in order to be good for them. They will need you, Cash. They will need a father who isn't dwelling on what's been ruined but what has been created.

You're going to need to be selfless, not selfish. You're going to need to put them first, not yourself. You have to stop focusing on the way you've been hurt or how shit didn't work out for you. Drink a fucking beer and move fucking on. Harsh, I know, but sometimes you need to hear the things people want to say to you but don't because they are afraid of hurting your feelings. I've never really cared about your feelings, have I?

You're a dweller. You dwell and think too much. You have to get over it; you have to move on. It's the only way to be happy, Cash. I want you to be happy. I want you to be a good father to the twins. I want you to love someone who will love you back. But you won't do that if you dwell on the things that can't be changed. Make peace with this, Cash. Make peace with yourself, and make peace for your children's sake.

You're lucky. You're going to see them grow; you're going to see them turn over, crawl, take their first steps. I don't want you to miss out on the good things I have brought to you because you couldn't get over the ruin I caused you.

You're going to be able to kiss all their boo-boos better. You're going to be their father that they look up to, learn from, who they brag to the kids at school about. You're going teach them to ride bikes and eat ice cream cones. You're going to play with them and tell them bedtime stories. You're going to be their leader. Lead them with laughter, and love. Not with ruin, Cash.

I'm so jealous that you get to be real to them. I won't be, just something that they hear stories about. I'm so afraid that you don't have any good stories to tell them. Make shit up if you have to; tell them the good stuff, Cash, that I loved to draw. You can tell them that I always wanted to go to art school. Make sure to tell them to do the things they want to do and not wait to do it. I wish I would have gone to art school. I should have gone.

If the twins show a creative side, involve them in the arts. Take them to classes; let them explore their gift. I saw that you started to draw. I peeked in your drawer and saw your sketches. You're really good. I never knew you could draw. Does your family know? Don't hide your gift. Be proud.

This is going to be hard, Cash, but life's hard.

Kennedy

CHAPTER 10

Bitter is the Taste that Lingers

The sun's bright, but the rays are filtered through the tint in the windows. I still feel as if I am burning up when Cassius pulls out his phone and I have to watch in horror as Hazel's number is tapped in painfully slow. The seatbelt cuts into my chest when I try leaning forward to hear her talk on the other end.

"You should call her later when you're alone." Caleb sounds dry, like he needs another juice box—his eyes find mine before looking back at the road.

"I want to speak to her." Cassius runs his finger over the image of her eyes, like something that is holy and divine, as he waits for her to answer her phone.

"Is this Hazel?" He uses a voice that I'm not familiar with; it sounds cold. I shiver.

"I want an appointment." There's a flex in Cassius's jaw while I slump into the seat.

"Tommie referred me. He gave me your business

card." A pause while he listens to a voice I can't hear on the other end.

"Tommie said to ask for the discount." He pulls the phone from his ear. I can hear her voice that has risen, but I can't make out the words.

"Do I get a discount?" he asks again, and this time I can hear Hazel on the other end.

"No discounts! Tommie has no idea what he's talking about. He doesn't know me or my work, but I promise after we're done, you will have a new understanding of what I do." Hazel's voice seems to raise the hackles between Cassius's shoulder blades. I can see the ridge fur trying to poke through.

Cassius's face drops lower than Hazel's voice just did as he listens to her, and my gut drops like I'm falling from somewhere high. I might get sick. A window rolls down while fresh air pushes in.

"Book me a spot." There is a wait. He taps the card, and the frown slides away, replaced with something dark, cunning.

"Saturday, seven. See you then, Hazel." He hangs up, raises up slightly in the seat to push the card into his back pocket.

"You're really going to meet her in Vegas?" Caleb's eyes shift to the side at Cassius. I watch him through the rearview mirror.

"Yes, I am. I just have to find where she's staying at."

"Wait, so you're going to Vegas, you don't know where she's at, and you're going to show up there at seven?" Caleb shakes his head.

"I'm going on a hunt. It shouldn't be that hard to track her." There is an uprise to his voice; the beat of my heart follows the sound of him upwards.

"What about the twins?"

Cassius gives him big eyes. "That won't work on me, brother. You're not Dee." Caleb huffs out.

"Please, only for the weekend."

"Why do you want to do this?"

"I need to, I don't know, I just need to go. I—" Cassius looks out the window, not able to finish his sentence—mouth clamped tight.

"So you're going to pay someone to fuck you? I'm sure you can find a willing female in the pack to help you out with that, brother."

"They don't look like her. They don't have those eyes."

Pain eats up my throat. I try to swallow; I try to blink it away. Nothing happens. It's still there, eating at me raw.

"Those eyes are a fucking problem—they don't belong to Kennedy. They belong to a female named Hazel, and the impression I get is that not a lot of people like Hazel. That is a fucking problem." I've never heard Caleb cuss so much. Usually, he never cusses, but right now, I think he's really angry. He's angry at Cassius.

"Will you take the kids for the weekend?" He avoids everything Caleb just said and continues to look out the window. The sun is so bright, yet inside here it feels like everything is shadowed in soggy dampness. I'm starting to sweat.

"I'll take the kids, but I don't agree with this."

"Thank you."

"What will you tell Mom and Dad?"

"That I need to get away for the weekend."

"Well, Mom's going to sniff around *that,* won't she?"

"I suppose, but I'm hoping you'll take her off the trail." Cassius doesn't plead; he just asks straightforward. I press a flattened out hand against the window. It's cool on the inside even though the outside is hot. I'm still sweating, though.

"You're going alone, right?" There is a hush to Caleb's voice.

"Yes, I'm going alone." Cassius's words retreat, quiet and slow.

Once again Caleb's eyes search into mine. His fingers tap against the steering wheel. "Good," he says as a final word.

"I don't think this is going to be a mistake." Cassius goes silent after he says that, and Caleb doesn't speak, either. My bones ache like someone just swallowed away my marrow.

"I don't know about that, but to each their own." Caleb presses his point but continues to stare forward, not making eye contact with me. The rest of the ride home I stare out the window, with my head pressed against the glass. It's a struggle not to cry.

The sun's rays don't penetrate through the windows. It's dim, dark almost. It reminds me of how Belac found me. It was so bright outside, but in the culvert, it was shadowy with a muggy heat. I didn't know then, but she saw a picture of me in the paper scavenging for food at the dump with the article saying the wolf population in the area has increased. It went on to include tips on how to keep your pets safe.

112

Belac immediately knew what I was, and she came every day with fresh meat. Raw and blood-soaked. She was patient, and eventually, she won trust with a soft-spoken voice and gentle hands. The food helped, too. I didn't shift right away. I followed her home; the walk was slow because I couldn't see very good.

We ran into a male. Later I found out it was her brother crossing into her territory. I've never seen *Wilds* fight before, but when her brother said she should show me mercy and put me down, Belac sprung and was on him with teeth. The sounds they made had me running and running back to the culvert, to the security of being underground. I didn't come back out until I heard Belac outside the tunnel. She was beaten really bad; she was dragging her hind leg that was almost torn off. She didn't shift to the skin; she stayed in the cocoon of fur. She curled up in a ball. It rained that night, and I thought she was going to drown when the water started to get deeper. I tried to move her with teeth, but it was too hard.

There was no choice but to shift from fur to skin, dragging her out of the water with my fingers clinging into the scruff of her neck. I tried to scream for help, but nothing would come out. I found out that my voice was gone.

Belac shifted from her cocoon of fur to skin. She regarded me with rain dripping into her eyes. She screamed as if in real pain, but I didn't see her get hurt again. Her arms opened up wide, and I stepped into them, naked and soaking wet.

We were skin to skin.

She rocked me. "No more," she said. "No more. You're safe now." She said it like a promise, and I closed my eyes and wanted to believe the promise.

The sound of the door closing scatters the memories away.

"Treajure, give me your glasses." Cassius is blurry, and I have to find my glasses that are on my lap.

He's quiet for a moment, and I can hear him play with the arms of the glasses. "The screw is a little loose on the right side. I'll fix them when we get home." He hands them back to me like it's no big deal that he's become the caretaker of my glasses. He bought a repair kit, and he's always making sure they fit properly. He likes to take them off my face so he can clean them and make sure none of the screws have become wobbly. Cassius will spend a half hour sometimes on them, making sure everything is just right, but what I like most is when he puts them back on my face.

He'll curl the hair around my ear, and his thumb runs along my earlobe. My skin felt the shock the first time he did that; it seemed to shiver on its own. He would get all the strands away from my face, his breath would change, and I inhaled as he exhaled the word *perfect* once they were properly placed on my face. Sometimes his hands will linger on my shoulders before he pulls them away and shoves them in his pockets. One day, I want to tell him thank you. One day.

Caleb comes back into the van, and Cassius hands the glasses back to me.

"Pictures are mailed." Caleb sounds giddy

almost.

Cassius shakes his head. "Those aren't for me, right?"

"No, they're for Clayton. I had an exceptional shit this morning, and I couldn't help taking a few eight by ten glossies."

"You've got real issues, Caleb. No one wants to see your shit." Cassius pulls a nasty grimace across his face; even my nose wrinkles up.

"Well, when you shit as good as I do, you'll be sending pictures."

"Do you have another juice box?" Cassius asks.

"You know I keep this van stocked." Caleb reaches underneath the seat and hands him one.

Cassius takes the straw out of the package, plunges the straw inside the carton, and hands it to me before he asks for another one.

I sip it slowly while Cassius sucks it back in a swallow.

Entering the house, Luna Grace is there with Dee at the table coloring.

"Where were you guys?" Luna Grace asks as she gets up from the table.

"I missed you." Dee's lips are already pushed out for a kiss from her dad. He gives her a kiss and asks how her morning was.

"Treajure, sit by me. Watch me." I sit with her in the middle of her dad and me. I can't help leaning my nose in and smelling the pup. A few strands have fallen in her eyes, and I smooth them down so they're out of her way. Rubbing her back, my hand accidentally brushes over Cassius, and he pauses and gives a small grunt in the back of his throat before moving his hand away from mine. He picks up a crayon and begins to draw a picture in the corner of the page she's working on.

"Mom, I'm going out of town this weekend." Cassius doesn't look up as he tells his mother this. He's working intently on the picture he's drawing as his daughter is trying to stay in the lines of what she's coloring. Cassius made all their coloring books, and now he sells them online as well.

"Where are you going?"

"Caleb's going to watch them for me."

"Where are you guys going?"

"Guys?" Cassius looks a little confused.

"You and Treajure?"

"What...no. I'm going alone."

"Where are you going all alone?" The Luna stops everything she's doing to turn toward Cassius.

"I need to get away for the weekend." He won't make eye contact with his mother. He draws with total concentration.

"Mom, I need your help." Caleb winks at Cassius when his head raises up.

"What, Caleb?" There is suspicion in her voice.

"Clayton's looking for a Beta. Could you put out some feelers, see if there are any takers, something?"

The crayon in Cassius's hand snaps, and Dee jumps slightly, looking confused. I can even feel the tension coming from between Cassius's shoulder blades as he stiffens up.

"Yes, I could make a few phone calls. I'll ask my sister to put her feelers out, too." She walks by Cassius and kisses him on the top of his head before looking out the window.

"I'm not sure how much luck we will have. No Beta will want to leave their pack willingly to go to Clayton's. The Beta he gets will be troubled. He's not wanted in his pack for one reason or another. Are you sure Clayton understands what he might be getting?" Luna Grace's words warn while she turns from the window to access Caleb.

"And Clayton's not troubled? I guess they will be a perfect match." Caleb walks over to his mother and puts his arm over her shoulder and gives her a side hug. She looks up at him and shakes her head.

"Thanks, Mom." He bends to rest his cheek against the top of her head.

"You want to go check on Mrs. Oink?" Cassius asks Dee, and she's already running to get her boots on. It rained three days ago, but she needs them to not get dirty. When he brought home their rain boots, both Ken and Dee wouldn't take them off, and Cassius got the hose out so they would have puddles to splash in that afternoon. He even brought me a pair that day so I could splash with them. He laughed at us playing in the water as he sat against the tree with his sketch book. When I went to bed that night, I didn't let the smile slip off my face when I scooted underneath the wood frame after Cassius asked me, "Do you need anything, Treajure?"

"Specs, you coming?" Dee's small hand stretches out to mine before she goes outside. When I look up at Cassius, he nods his head that it's all right to come. I don't want to intrude on their times, but the way she's smiling, I don't want to say no, so

I get up, put on my matching boots, and walk outside with them to the farm.

Cassius is humming a song under his breath.

Letter 10

Cash,

You tried to kiss me last night. You were so close, then what happened? You pulled away, turned away, walked away.

I would have let you kiss me. A real kiss— is that what you were going to do? Give me some kind of romantic kiss? I was waiting for it. You couldn't deliver.

Remember the first time you kissed me? I bit your lip, and you bit me right back. We both were left blood-smeared. I've never been handled that way, so rough and uncaring. Then again, I've never handled anyone as rough as I handled you. I've never been so terrified of someone before. You terrified me, and I can see how I terrified you.

You caught me hiding on the island. You hunted me like some kind of animal. I'm not an animal. I'm not anything you accused me of being that day. You were so angry, Cash. So very very angry, and I wanted you to become enraged. I wanted you to be the monster I was accusing you of being. I know I

118

brought you over the edge when I pointed to the spot where I lost my virtue to Clayton. I wanted you to go there so I could say you're pathetic, I could say you are everything I accused you of. So I told you how good it was to have an Alpha between my legs; I told you that you couldn't compare to him. You could never be him and that I will never forget this spot. You could do anything you wanted to me, but I would never forget that spot. I would never forget Clayton. I told you that when you kissed me, it would be Clayton I will pretend to kiss. When you fuck me, I would be fucking Clayton, never you. You got so quiet, didn't you? So fucking quiet that I knew I pushed you over the edge and I was happy I did it.

I could feel your rage, and I loved it. I was so happy when you pulled me into your arms and tried to kiss Clayton out of me. I bit you so hard, and I told you that the only way to get me is to force yourself on me. That you are a weak little wolf who even a mate doesn't want to fuck. I laughed at you and told you only weak wolves force themselves on weaker wolves.

I watched how you lost your balance. You sat down on a log with mushrooms growing from the decaying trunk. You were a massive dick, and I was a massive cunt. I'm just saying the truth of how it was in the beginning for both of us. I know you'll agree with that.

You couldn't get up, so I ran as fast as I could and remembered being so tired when I tried to swim to shore. I was so tired, and when I started going underwater, it felt peaceful when I did slip lower and lower without the noise, without the fear; everything was calming once I let go of the fear of dying. I chose death than to be without Clayton, but you had to come and rescue me, you had to take that peace away, and I was such a bitch to you after that.

I could get underneath your skin, couldn't I? All I had to do is mention something and you'd balance on that edge. Swaying.

Back then I hated you so much, but I hated Rya so much more. I fucking hated her for coming back, for being some kind of fucking miracle that everyone felt sorry for. There was nothing I could do about Rya, but I could hurt you. I could hurt you so I could feel better.

I won't lie, fighting Rya that day felt so fucking good. She threw bread at me, and I almost laughed out loud. Bread. Of all the things she could have thrown and she picked bread. She might have got me good a few times, but I was kicking her ass. If we weren't split apart, I would have killed her that day. I would have, and I don't think I would have even felt bad about it. Would I regret it? Fuck no. The look Dallas gave me was intense. You stepped in front of that look. He hates me. I can see it in his eyes. He hates me. I think he's a fucking dick for fucking with Rya in the first place.

It drove Clayton insane when he finally figured it out between Dallas and Rya. I mean, we ate at Dallas's table and he ate at ours. We shared meals together. It pushed Clayton away from me, knowing that his mate had some wolf sniffing around her. We argued a lot. He even suggested that we break up. The bond was too much to fight anymore. He didn't want to hurt me; he didn't want to cheat on me or feel like he was cheating on me because he couldn't stop the way his entire nature wanted to be with Rya.

We started having the talk underneath an apple tree. I bought him that tree. Can you believe that? He always loved his garden, even as a little pup. It started off with Clayton needing to talk to me. He wanted to be

121

truthful. No lies. He put his hands on my shoulders, and I don't know if he was trying to steady me or me steadying him. He told me that he and Dallas had a fight and that he can't stay away from Rya. He can't fight the bond anymore. We had to break up, not because he doesn't love me, but because he loves me and respects me enough to understand that there was no more future with me anymore. Not when he couldn't get Rya out of his mind, out of his dreams. It was like she started to infect him and the only cure was her. My cure for him was to kill Rya. It was the only way. He could be free of the bond; his Wild would be free to love someone else.

Cash, I'm that monster. I am a monster. I started to tell Clayton that we could get through this, that we could overcome anything together, and he told me I didn't understand the pull of the bond. So I switched directions and asked him how is Rya going to love you after everything you've done to her? Now that question comes back to me. How can you try to love me after everything I've done to you?

Kennedy

CHAPTER 11

Lingers on the Edge of Change

The sky looks light grey, or maybe it's blue…I'm not sure, but I wave good-bye with the twins as we watch Cassius pull out of the driveway early Friday morning. He couldn't sleep last night, and neither could I. He tossed, I turned. I heard every shift of the mattress above me, every huff of breath. I heard him get up a few times to get a glass of water then back to bed. I couldn't even look at him this morning, no matter how hard he tried to make me look at him. He packed his bags and I've packed mine.

At the beginning of the week when the twins were asleep, he remained hunched over his computer, searching, tracking this Hazel until he closed the screen down with victory spread across his face. "I got her, Specs," he said to me. I couldn't smile like he was.

He went shopping by himself, and when he came home, he gave Ken and Dee some new pajamas for their sleepover they were going to have with Uncle Caleb this weekend. He even bought me the match to Dee's pajamas—she likes it when we match. I couldn't resist peeking in the closet. My heart dropped when I unzipped the bag with a brand new suit inside it. He even bought new shoes and something to make him smell good. I've never seen Cassius wear a suit, ever. I went to bed before him that night. I slid under the bed and told myself I shouldn't be underneath here anymore. It's not right for him or for me. This was just a big game of pretending.

If it's time for him to change, maybe it's time I should, too. I'm not his wish. I was never his wish like he was mine.

Last night, he packed his bag, and I took out my earrings. They were only in there for him, and I have to stop making up stories that he'll notice them on me. He won't. So I put them back into the soft velvet case they came in. My weekend bag is packed, and a part of me wants to take all my belongings out of my room and bring them to Caleb's house. I don't because Belac is coming back, and they don't need me in their space when she finally comes back.

"Treajure, that's a lot of bags for a weekend." Caleb picks up the two backpacks with worry spelled in the furrows between his eyebrows.

"You plan on staying for a while?" I shake my head no to him.

Luna Grace looks at my ears and stops everything she's doing.

"Where did Cash go, Caleb?" Luna Grace asks

124

very clearly.

"I'm not too sure. He said he needed to get away." He gives an unclear answer. Caleb backs up because Luna Grace leans in on him.

"Where did your brother go?"

"He went to Vegas to meet up with Hazel." Caleb can't keep anything private. A little muscle and he squeals as if he's been shanked with hot silver.

"He went to Vegas to meet Hazel?" Luna Grace takes a step back, concerned now.

"It was something he said he had to do."

"What did he have to do?" Luna Grace steps into Caleb's space and backs him against the wall. He can't escape.

"I don't know, Mom. What do you think he went to do in Vegas with Hazel?"

Luna Grace takes a big breath, looks up at the ceiling, lets the air out slowly, and pauses to regard me.

"Is that why you're not wearing your earrings anymore, Treajure? You're upset he went to Vegas to meet Hazel?"

It's impossible to answer her the way I want to. I want to say that I have to change. I have to change, and I can't keep pretending that Cassius is mine. He's not. He never was, and now I think it's best to put away those earrings that were bought on a whim and a wish. I really thought he would notice me wearing them. All he did was faintly grunt in his throat and look up at the ceiling as if searching for something. I have to stop pretending. I have to try to sleep in my own bed. It would be weird sleeping underneath his bed if he brings Hazel back here. I couldn't handle it if I saw them kiss or if the kids started to love her. It would kill me slowly to see her give him the things I could never, like sleeping on a bed with him or answering a question he asks. Hazel is beautiful, and so was Kennedy. He has tastes that I can't fulfill for him. I'm not blind; I know what I look like. It's just Cassius made me feel important. Beautiful even. He made me feel like a full-grown female. At times I even felt I had breasts because I caught him a few times letting his eyes drop lower than my mouth. I felt on fire those times, and he would be so close to me, and his voice would drop, and I would think he might kiss me. He never did.

Luna Grace curses underneath her breath. She never swears. Ever.

"Why aren't you wearing your earrings?" She doesn't lean into me when she asks, but my glasses still fall to the floor. She bends down to pick them up and puts them back on my face. She kisses my forehead near the hairline; I see her kiss Rya this way, and before Belac left for the Wilds, she gave her a kiss like this as well.

"Sometimes I think Cassius can't see what's in front of his face."

"That's about right," Caleb states while going after the kids who have already hopped into the van.

"It looks like you're changing, Treajure." Luna Grace stops me from going out the front door.

I nod my head yes.

"You need to do what feels right for you, Treajure. You will always have a place with us even

126

if you think this isn't right for you." Her voice seems choky wet.

My cheek nudges hers before a hard press that lasts a long time, with my arms wrapped around her in a hug. I don't cling to her like I used to. Instead, I hug her and she hugs me back.

"I understand, Treajure. There's only so much a wolf can take. I understand. I hope Cassius will, too. We can't force wolves in the directions we want them to go. We can nudge them, we can try to guide them, but we can't force anything they're not ready for. I'm proud of the direction you're going in. You've come a long way." Once again, she kisses my forehead and smooths down my hair. I can feel her hand slide all the way to my lower back before she lets me go. I'm not sure, but why does this feel like some sort of goodbye?

"You've come a long way since I first met you." She takes my hand in hers. "You've grown into a beautiful wolf. I consider you one of my own. No matter what happens, I consider you mine." A claw comes out, and she holds my chin so I look right into her eyes.

"Maybe this is for the best. Sometimes wolves don't understand what they have until it's gone. He will notice...don't think he won't. He will notice, and don't make it easy for him, Treajure. Make him work for what he wants, because in my heart I know he wants you." She presses her cheek to mine once again before letting me go.

"Specs, let's roll," Ken hollers as the sliding door to the van shuts.

The music is not too loud, but loud enough for

the twins' ears. They are singing along to the song from one of their movies. Caleb is singing too as he backs up.

"First, who needs a juice box?"

Both of the twins raise their hands and say, "Me!"

"We are loaded up today, Treajure. Everything we need for the farm." There is clapping, and the pups wiggle in their car seats.

"You like the farm, right?' I nod my head because I do love the farm. I like to watch them play with their father and take care of Mrs. Oink and Mr. Bill. We all do our chores together until we run in the wildflower field and drop in the middle underneath the only tree that grows there. A big willow tree that's dug its roots in a small pond its shade has created. We get to sit underneath the tree and have lunch that I made us. I know all their favorite foods and make sure we have lots of water so they don't get dehydrated. It's hard not to worry that they aren't drinking enough. It's some of my favorite times with them at the farm. Cassius once let me put my head on his lap when I felt so relaxed that I couldn't keep my eyes open. I fell asleep to his fingers running through my hair as I listened to the twins chase each other through the field. When I woke up from that nap, I couldn't believe I fell asleep out in the open like that. That never happened before. He put his sketchbook away when I lifted my cheek from his thigh. He pretended I didn't drool all over his worn jeans. They were threadbare in the spot my skin was pressed against, and I could feel his skin against mine.

"Are you all right, Treajure?" Caleb asks. I can't answer him. I'm not really all right, but what did I expect for being in love with a fantasy? I played at pretend, and now, I'm paying the price of realizing that it wasn't real.

"Hazel is not his type."

I'd like to ask Caleb what's Cassius's type is, but I think he's just doing it for my sake. Caleb turns up the movie in the back, down in the front.

"To tell you the truth, I don't think Hazel would be a good fit, and not because she works in Vegas. Everyone needs to earn a living. Cash doesn't need another Kennedy, and from what I've heard, she reminds me of Kennedy. He had that, and it was hard on everyone. We wanted to like her, we did. I couldn't love her. She was the vilest creature I have ever met. True story. Don't tell Cash. I told Clayton I didn't like Kennedy once, and he punched me in the face. I don't want to fight my brother. Kennedy isn't worth brothers to fight over." Caleb's voice is hushed as he looks in the review mirror at the kids, who are now eating crackers and drinking their juice boxes, watching their favorite movie. I can never work the controls back there, but Ken's mastered it.

"You know if you need somewhere to stay, you can come back?"

I reach out and pat him on his cheek.

"Will you shank me again?" His voice is a hard set of words. I shrug my shoulders, not knowing what to answer because I can't promise that.

Caleb throws his head back and laughs. I'd like to ask him if he really thinks Cassius will fuck

Hazel. I don't ask; I keep the questions to myself. Deep down I know what he's doing. Deep down I know.

Whenever we see someone he knows on the road, he waves and gives a honk.

"Who says you can't live your best life driving a minivan?" The windows are down, and he's smiling as if he owns the world.

Pulling up to the farm, Rya is standing there holding a bouquet of wildflowers. Her belly is slightly showing; she's having a female. It's the first time ever for a Valentine to have a female in their alpha line. Dallas puts Chance down to run toward the van when we stop.

Rya always smells better than the entire field of wildflowers. She makes me want to take big breaths in and out until I'm full of her scent. It tingles at my bones and makes me feel giddy, almost drunk, if I stay too long around her. Those are the times I want to kiss Cassius the most or touch him. My skin feels alive and excited when Cassius and Rya are out and I'm there with them. I get hungry, just not for food. For skin in my mouth, for teeth to scrape against flesh. For my tongue to taste him. Some other females say the same thing; they say they get horny for their mates being around Rya.

Cassius isn't my mate, but when I'm around Rya, he feels like he could be. Those tingles, the feeling of his eyes on me, his scent changes, and I can actually taste it at the back of my throat. Once Cassius put his arms around me and held me on his lap and told me I smelled different when we had a sleepover at Rya's house because Dallas was away at a seminar. He was stone hard underneath his pants. I felt it. His cock was hard, and I was on his lap. His hands were on my thighs, and I felt the shift of his hips. His breathing was hot, and I was on fire. Rya walked in on us and Cassius mumbled he had to go to bed. In the morning he said sorry that he had a lot to drink and it got away from him. Those words felt like an execution.

Cash hardly drank after that.

"Treajure, where are your earrings?" Rya curls my hair around my ear.

"Sore subject, Rya," Caleb answers for me.

"What happened?"

"Cash is an idiot." Caleb walks away, and Dallas and Rya are left staring at my face.

"I'm making wildflower soap today, Treajure. Do you want to help?" I nod my head with a smile, but a shriek from Ken has the *Wild* evacuate skin to fur with dizzying speed. The warrior goose has him lying on the ground as wings spread wide over the top of him. We smell Ken's blood, and there is an execution of a goose that stood no chance against the teeth of a *Wild*. She tears into the bird, she rips out its feathers, she tosses it in the air. The *Wild* disembowels the fowl.

When Caleb tries to approach, the *Wild* shows him blood-dripping teeth that are sharper than a silver shank.

"That was aggressive," Caleb says to chastise the *Wild*, but when he sees Ken's bloody knee, even he wears a white flash of teeth.

"Don't worry, Treajure, the goose had it coming," Dallas says as he picks up Ken in his arms and looks at his gravel-riddled hands and his torn-up knee. Ken is still screaming as if all his lifeblood is coming out of his body. He cries as if he's been torn apart.

"Ken, you get to choose the Band-Aid. Let's clean that up." Dallas has him in his arms—Dee and Chance are holding hands, following Dallas with concern in their eyes.

When Caleb tries to get close to the now torn apart goose, the *Wild* nips at his hand. Her kill, she won't release it. She might even eat the bones; that's how mad she is about Ken getting hurt on her watch.

We are left outside until nothing remains of the goose except feathers. Alpha Clinton has come to inspect the injured, and the *Wild* is so full she's laying belly up in the sun with her tongue hanging out. He bends down and takes her jaw in his hand; her teeth remain tucked in tight, just like her tail.

"Good job." He lets her face go, gives a quick scratch behind her ear, and walks toward the house. Ken has stopped crying, but his limp is excessive.

"Are you sure he didn't break his leg?" Caleb asks. Dallas doesn't answer him back.

"Good thing our little warrior was here." Alpha Clinton picks up Ken and holds him to him, smelling his neck with a small bite to his shoulder that doesn't break the skin.

The *Wild* is full, Ken is safe, and her Alpha just called her little warrior. Her life is simple, and she rests in the sun, soaking up the rays, keeping one eye on the twins, content and happy.

Letter 11

Cash,

You asked me what was wrong last night before bed. I wanted to tell you, "Everything." Everything is wrong; this entire situation between us is wrong. I'm wrong. You're fucking wrong for not giving up on me. I'm not someone you should fight for, Cash. I'm not worth your fight. Instead of telling you what's wrong, I faced the wall and pretended to fall asleep. You turned your back, pressed your spine against mine, and fell asleep for real.

I'm afraid Clayton will forget about me in time. He's going to forget about us and how much I loved him. I don't want to be forgotten by him, and it kills me inside that I might be. I'm afraid for him to move on, and what's really screwed up is that I want you to forget about me. Forget about all of this; turn this into some kind of obscure dream that you can wake up and move on from.

I was tired today. I'm so tired. It was hard to lift the paintbrush, so you took it from my hand and finished the spot I was working on. You've gotten so good. I think in time, you'll be a better artist than me. You should practice in all mediums, clay, charcoal, acrylics...try woodworking or stonework. I think you could be good at anything. It just takes time and patience, and I know you've got patience.

If the twins show promise in their art, cultivate it. Praise them and make them feel as if what they are doing is something meaningful and not just stupid drawings that will never amount to anything. My parents never supported my art; they didn't think it was something you could make a living off of. I never went to art school. I should have gone. I was afraid to be away from Clayton, and he was afraid for me to be away from him. He didn't support me going, so I stayed home.

That is a big regret in my life. I should have gone. I should have left and gone to art school instead of staying in the pack. Maybe we would have met under different circumstances? You can't go back in time. You can only go forward until your time is up. I really don't have much time left. You know it. I can see the devastation in your eyes.

Whenever I bring it up, you shut me up. You can't talk about it, and I can't bear to see that look in your eyes. Life's not fair. You want the things you can't have, and I want the things I can't have, either. It's not easy, Cash. This isn't easy on me, I know you want me to be stronger, to fight harder, but I'm too tired to want things anymore.

I heard your mother on the phone with Caleb. I guess Rya cheated on Dallas with Clayton. She's not so perfect now, is she? Your mother turned to your father and told him Dallas is coming home by himself.

That's what made me really upset today. Dallas is coming back, and I don't like your brother at all. I don't like the way he looks at me. I don't like Caleb, either. He's an asshole. A giant asshole who thinks he's this masterpiece of a wolf. He's not a masterpiece. He's a masterpiece of shit. You know he called me a bitch to my face, and maybe I deserved it, but fuck him for saying it. He's no different than me in a way; he's fucked females that aren't his mate, yet he judges me but can be friends with Clayton? I don't want the twins around him.

Carson, I'm neutral towards, and Crane is a disgusting little mess of a wolf. I'm afraid your brothers aren't going to be good for the twins to be around. They don't like me, and what happens if they don't like the twins because they come from me?

You're all they're going to have. Protect them, Cash. Protect them from things that they don't even know they need protecting from.

Everyone feels sorry for Dallas. I don't. He had to have known it was coming. How could Rya resist someone like Clayton? How? Rya's a cheater. Your good friend is a cheater, but you still love her like a sister. She cheated on your brother, but you still consider her a friend, but you can't see how Caleb can like Clayton? Ask yourself some meaningful questions, Cash. Ask yourself why you can be friends with a cheater who devastated your brother, but Caleb can't be friends with Clayton?

Double standards. Your family loves Rya, but they hate me? I know, a different situation, but I think even if I was to live, I'll only be tolerated by your family, not loved. Only tolerated.

Clayton's mother used to love me. We would go everywhere together. Our mothers were best friends. She loved me so much, and I loved her, I think, more than my mother. That all changed when Clayton knew I wasn't his mate. Everything changed that day we told them we weren't mates. From then on, I was *only tolerated by her, never loved again.*

The fights we would get into, the way his mother would drag her eyes down me whenever she saw us hugging or kissing. It's like she wanted to throw up and she blamed me for everything. I heard her talking about me and how her son was pussy-whipped. I wanted to yell at her that it wasn't my pussy he loved; it was me. Me. I didn't. I kept it to myself and tried to be this perfect wolf without any flaws, but she'd paw at me constantly. Nothing I did was ever good enough. Ever.

She would brag sometimes about Rya at the dinner table right in front of me, how proud that she's become a midwife and that she would be a contributing member of the pack. Clayton stood up for me then and said he's never going to sit at their table again if she can't stop talking about Rya. Clayton didn't want to hear about Rya; he didn't give a shit. His mother blamed me for their distance. I was blamed for everything. Loving Clayton was the easy part. It was everyone else that made things hard between us.

Sometimes I catch your mother watching me, and I don't have this need to be perfect. I'm just me, and for the first time in a long time, it feels good not to have to act that I don't make mistakes. Your mother's nice. We got off to a rocky start, but I understand that you're her child and she will protect you, even from your own mate.

Your father hardly speaks to me, but when he does, it has a lot of layered meaning that hits me at odd times, and I might laugh out loud or cry from it. He's a good father. I think you'll be like him. I hope you will be like him. I want you to be like him.

I never thought my life would turn out this way, and I bet you never thought your life would turn out this way, too.

Kennedy

CHAPTER 12

Change is a Grief-eater

Cassius

The men in the bar eat up Hazel with their eyes as if she's some sort of raw meat that's prepackaged in a form-fitting black dress.

"Do you know who that is?" I ask the bartender.

"Her name's Hazel. She's a freelancer."

Hazel makes her way to a table filled with pretty women and men in suits that don't hide their distended guts. The smell of money drips off them like water. Those eyes are exactly like Kennedy's. I breathe, once, twice, a third time before the smoke-filled air burns my lungs, and I want to choke on the thought that this might be another bad choice.

"What does that mean, freelancer?"

"See those girls at that table? Most work for the lady sitting by the stage in the blue dress. Hazel is her own employer. She's an independent."

This female I'm looking at doesn't seem like the

same one who sat across from me at the house with her eyes half-closed, mumbling. This female seems composed and well made up. She places ice at the bottom of the heavy glass and uncorks the whiskey bottle, filling the cup only enough to get a few swallows down.

"Does she come here a lot?"

"Once a month like clockwork."

"What's she like?"

"She's quiet, she doesn't cause any trouble unless someone messes with her, and when they do, she fucks them up."

"She fights?"

"No one will mess with her anymore, not even him." He nudges his chin toward a man near a door watching with his back leaning against the wall.

"Who is that?"

"No one you want to know." The hinges on the bartender's jaw flex.

"If you don't mind me asking, who let you in here?"

"Who let me in?" I try to play it off.

"You don't fit the clientele here."

"Are you profiling me?" I point my beer toward him before taking another sip.

"Yes, yes, I am."

"I slipped in. I've never been to Vegas, let alone VIP. I wanted to see if it was like the movies." Taking another sip of beer, I still watch Hazel in the mirror.

The bartender laughs. "It's nothing like the movies. It's better."

"So far, not impressed."

"Wait till Hazel goes on. Most of these men came for her."

"She strips?"

"I like the term visual artist," he corrects me respectfully.

A man pats his thigh, and Hazel sits on his lap, like some sort of pet. It's hard to finish the rest of the beer when she puts her glass to his lips and he finishes the rest of her drink. She nudges him with her nose before leaving behind the smudge of red against his neck.

Hazel spreads her legs, and the man's hand disappears underneath the hem of her dress. Her mouth is parted slightly and her eyes de-focus. Is she enjoying the man pawing her?

"Have you slept with her?"

"I tried, not enough cash in the wallet. Hazel does nothing for free."

The more the man finger fucks her, the more straight whiskey she drinks. She doesn't even use ice. She's watching the new dancer on stage, and the man is watching his finger sliding in and out of her. Hazel drinks more and more, and the man mauls between her legs.

The back of Hazel's head is leaned against his shoulder, her back is arched, and her hips shift slightly. At first, I think she might be enjoying it, but all I can see are hollow hazel eyes.

"Hey buddy, she's out of your league. See those women over there? Those are more your style. Hazel's premium."

She gets up and takes the stage. Red flashes from the bottom of her shoes.

Her nose lifts in the air, her eyes find mine, and I give her a little nod to say hello. There is something rancid that traces along her lip line. Turning around to fully face her, I lean back. If she's putting on a show, who am I not to watch?

She stiffens up for a second before I see the roll of her shoulders. Her eyes go blank, and she moves to the ghostly rhythm of the song. Her eyes re-focus on the man in the chair, and all the men are concentrating on Hazel. The women try to look unimpressed but fail.

Hazel owns the space of the stage; she moves, and the crowd shifts in their seats. I can even hear some of them gasp when she slides that dress down her body slowly until she steps out of it with only a bra and panties and those red bottom shoes.

Her red shade of lipstick matches the shoes. It's a startling combination; the eye traces up to her lips, down to her feet. Up and down, she's gorged by eyes that can't look away. The man leaning against the wall looks at Hazel like she's prey, that he's going to devour this beauty and spit her out in pieces. A part of me wants to throw him through the window, but this might be what Hazel wants, to be eaten up like this. Who am I to interfere with her business?

I've never seen a female so confident. She sculpts beauty with movement.

Taking another sip of beer, feeling the way the cold liquid slides down my throat, I'd like to fuck Hazel, but that thought fades away because the *Wild* won't have any of that. He's giving me what I need, but he won't let me take anything more than tomorrow night. I'm not here for Hazel. I'm here for something else.

The bartender has stopped making drinks. I can hear him exhale behind my right shoulder. We both watch the Hazel show, breathing a little harder as she spins herself around the pole, spreading her legs as wide as she can. Those shoes flashing red, her red lips are licked by her tongue, making them wet. Glistening.

I'm glad Hazel kept her bra and panties on. I didn't want to see her naked. Not yet. She slips that dress back on, and the man leads her away like some kind of dog owner. She's allowing herself to be owned. It's hard not to stalk behind them. I can see Hazel's tension stiffen her spine ramrod straight. She doesn't like me at all.

There is no eye contact between us, nothing as I walk by. She knows I'm here, and that's all that needed to be said. For now.

The cab ride is short back to the hotel. Traffic blurs; lights are too bright. A sinking feeling settles in my gut when I open the door up to my room. The box sits on the bed, waiting for me to fill it up with Kennedy's things. A gut pain folds me up before it goes away and I can stand straight again.

This could be another bad choice in a long line of bad choices, but somehow it feels right. Needed.

The red dress is first to be put in, air sealed with her pillowcase so Kennedy's scent never fades away. I gave the twins every piece of her clothing when they were born to wrap around them, so they could smell their mother. When the scent faded, I threw it out and used a new shirt or pants, anything that held her scent. After a few months, nothing was left but the red dress, and I couldn't let go of it. Until now.

Red bra and panties that she never wore but were in her underwear drawer. They smell of her, and I seal them up as well. Her makeup I threw out except for the red lipstick that she would wear at times when she didn't go downstairs. She loved makeup but refused to wear it after a while. She stopped caring about herself, and when I stopped feeling sorry for myself, it was too late for her to want to care about anything.

A simple note on the top of the pile.

Hazel,

No other scents on you but hers. See you at seven.

Cash.

Jazz music plays low in the lobby as I wait for Hazel to come back from her evening adventures. The box is at my feet while I sketch a picture for the new coloring book, but once I'm done with it, I start to draw *her.* My hands can't stop interacting with her in some way, even if it's drawing her silhouette, the bridge of her nose, her simple smile.

It's three a.m. by the time she comes back. She's not as made up as she was in the club; her hair's messy, her walk is sloppy, and she looks to be in some form of pain. She doesn't notice me while pressing the button for the elevator.

Right before the door closes, I slide in, and that rancid look comes back to her face. I press the floor number, and she swipes her card. Penthouse.

"Wolf, I'm tired. I need to go to bed." Whiskey

lingers on her breath, and blood is smelled on her skin. There's suffering held in her eyes.

"Me too. I've been waiting for you for a long time now."

She sneers with eyes that maul. "Why?"

"I needed to make sure you got this. It's for our date at seven." I hand her the box. "I have instructions in there what I want you to do. I expect them to be followed." My eyes don't waver from hers.

She leans into me, box touching my waist. "Are you sure about this, Wolf? You might not like what's waiting for you when I open the door to greet you at seven. It won't be her standing there smiling. It will be me."

"I understand that, Hazel. I just want those directions followed. I'm paying for that." Pushing pointed words into her, she doesn't flinch.

The elevator dings, the door opens, and I step out.

"Make sure to ask the front desk to let you up. I'll tell them I'm expecting you." The door closes, I go my way, and she goes hers.

Letter 12

Cash,

We never got the chance to undress ourselves, did we?

Don't be afraid to undress yourself in front of someone special, who will appreciate the way your bones are nicked. You're not broken, just ruined. There's a big difference.

It's hard at times to look at you because your pain echoes inside me. It hurts. You hurt—we both hurt for different reasons—but it's still pain.

I woke up earlier than you today. Your cock was pressed against my ass. Rock hard and hungry. But you never make a move between us. I know your body aches for me. I can smell it on you when you think I'm still asleep in the morning and you have your nose pressed against the back of my neck. Inhaling. Your desire stretches at the insides of me. I ache sometimes for your cock, I do. Surprised, right? It would feel good to be filled up, to hold onto your neck, your arms as you fuck me.

Our first time together doesn't really count, does it? We were angry at each other, you more so than me. I still can remember your face when I got out of that place and showed up where you were. I would have never been able to get out and track you if we weren't mates. You're able to draw and I'm able to hunt. So weird these talents we pick up from the other.

You grabbed my arm and started to drag me back, and I stopped you with a hand on your chest. You didn't really want to take me back. I could see the bulge in your pants; you were panting and dripping. I've never experienced that kind of smell before, the leaking of a male wolf. I'm already getting wet thinking back on it.

I put my hands on you for the first time not to hit, but to feel you, and you let me, reluctantly, but you let me feel your chest, and I felt you shake underneath my hands. I couldn't stop myself when I rubbed you through your jeans. I knew exactly what I was doing, and you, you had no chance against what I was doing. Those hormones drive you to do things you never thought you would ever do.

You told me how wrong this would be, that you needed to take me home, but my hand was there making you stay in your spot. You never had a female's hand on your cock before. You had plenty of opportunities, but you always would make some sort of excuse to those females.

My hand kept all your excuses quiet that day, didn't it? You wanted to protest, but your cock was rebelling against your mind. Your cock won for the first time, didn't it?

The power shifted, didn't it, Cash? I brought you right there to the edge, and then stopped and we collided together, all teeth and blood.

Not a proper kiss, we never had one of those, but fuck, it was hot. I will give you that; we were all a gnash of teeth and tongues and so so angry. Both of us.

I bit you, and you bit me right back.

You turned me around because I told you I didn't want to see your face when you fucked me. That was a lie, but I wanted you to be as angry as I was. I had no control, and in a way, I stopped all your control too. That made you angry, so you pressed me against the wall and tore at my pants. I wasn't wearing underwear and you lost your shit, didn't you?

It was so long since I had sex that when you rammed inside of me I swear I thought I would split open, and all the nasty things you said—I lost my shit too. I came so hard that you had to hold me up off the ground with your cock so far inside me I swear I could gag on the tip.

You wanted to fuck Clayton out of me, and in that moment, you did. I couldn't think of him. All I thought about was you and how our bodies fit perfectly. How your hands were so rough and my skin would remember every spot you held. It was like our bones were trying to find each other.

I bit my way along your arm and you left

your mark across my shoulder. You fucked me with this insane anger, and with every thrust, I could feel you getting closer. I knew we were going to create something inside me. I didn't want it to stop no matter how much my mind wanted it to stop. My lust was too much to overcome. After you came, you stopped. You just stopped as if your head cleared, and you told me to get dressed, but you couldn't get out of me. Your Wild knotted himself up inside me and we were forced to stay together.

I shifted my hips and you groaned. What a fucking sound. I can still hear that sound in my dreams. You took me again, rougher than the last time. I swear I thought I was going to split open, but I didn't give a shit. All I wanted was you inside me, and I couldn't bear the thought of you getting out.

You took me with my hands pressed against the wall, and I was on my tiptoes, and those things you were saying, how you felt me come, that I didn't come that good for him. Fuck, you bit me again and again and again. It wasn't gentle, it was all anger and malice, and I loved every fucking minute. I felt you come; I felt every single squirting pulse inside me.

Still, the Wild would not release me, so we

fucked and fucked until I thought your heart would give out. When the door opened up and your parents looked at us as if we were doing something wrong, I wanted to crawl underneath you. Instead, you put me behind your back and told me to get dressed. We didn't see each other again until my heat died down, and when I saw you, I laughed in your face.

I lied to you, Cash. I lied and lied because I was upset with myself. I felt a lot of guilt because Clayton and I promised each other that there would be no others for us. We would be each other's first and last. Even though you were my mate, I felt as if I were cheating on Clayton. I felt sick and wanted you to feel sick too. I wanted to torture you. I managed to do a really good job of that, didn't I? The awful things I said, I didn't mean it, Cash. I didn't mean all of that. I wanted you to hurt. I needed you to hurt so I wasn't hurting alone.

That was about me. It was about me understanding how easy Clayton will be able to be with Rya if he gives himself the chance. I knew I'd only be a memory for him, eventually, and inside I was twisted up about it. Nothing good was inside me then, Cash. I blocked everything good up inside me so only the shit could spill and spew out of my mouth. Clayton was going to forget about me, and I couldn't handle it. I couldn't handle everything that happened, and you were there to take everything I could give you. Deep down, it was also me understanding that Clayton would become a memory for me the longer I stayed with you.

I'm sorry.

I just wish that things were different between us. I've silenced you, haven't I? You can't even really talk to me about anything because you think I will judge you, so you think it's better to keep quiet than open your mouth and talk to me. It's the same for me. I want to talk to you, but I just don't know how.

You put the cribs up today. I watched you work, and when you were finished, you had this smile on your face. A big proud smile that made you look like a juvenile wolf who just caught his first rabbit. When I didn't smile back, you lost that smile, and I should have said, good job—something, anything— but I didn't, and you walked out of the room with something throbbing inside your chest.

Sometimes I don't know how to say thank you. The words get stuck in my throat, and I can't seem to say anything, so I stay silent.

I'm quiet around you because I don't know what to really say to you, how to talk to you. What can we say that needs to be said? We both are weaved so tight into our skins that I don't think we could really undress ourselves to the other. So I'm writing as a way to show you my bones. It's not pretty. I'm not beautiful on the inside, am I?

Your insides are still good, Cash. They aren't twisted and blocked like mine; there's hope for you. Don't let this keep you twisted up or blocked from experiencing the life you should be living. I'm going to be the story you tell our children. Be kind to my memory with them. Kids need to feel like their mothers are good wolves, not some evil villain that gives them nightmares and fucks up their entire lives up.

Kennedy

CHAPTER 13

Grief-eater Consumes Regret

This is not another bad choice, I keep saying over in my head as I try not to loosen the tie that feels like a noose around my neck. The flowers smell sweet. They were her favorite flowers to draw. Kennedy learned how to sketch the wildflowers first before she moved onto more complicated things. It was the first thing I drew that felt right after her death.

Room service has left, and I count to three before knocking on the door. This is not a bad choice. When the door opens, it's hard not to freeze up.

She's dripping in red...

"You look beautiful." Stepping into her space, she smells exactly like Kennedy. Another inhale and I could stand here all day with my nose buried into her neck pretending. But this isn't about pretending; this is about good-bye.

"These are for you." I can't stop staring at her eyes; they look exactly like Kennedy's, except without the hurt.

It's a quick kiss I press against her lips, and she tastes exactly like Kennedy. I can't stop tasting my own lips now, with her scent on them.

"You look good, Cash. Please come in." Everything smells like her; everything in this room smells exactly like Kennedy. The low light plays tricks on my eyes, and I see the illusion of Kennedy smiling at me with red lips. Not Hazel.

"I hope you don't mind, but I ordered for you." Hazel makes it easy to forget she's here and I'm now with Kennedy. I drop the small bag near the door for later.

"No, I don't mind." She turns, leading me into a room where dinner is set up. Through the window, the city lights bleed into the night. The food is formal, elegant, and everything that Kennedy always wanted to try. Red wine is in the decanter.

"What's your Wi-Fi password?" She tells me, and I put on Kennedy's playlist through the system the penthouse comes with.

Pulling out the chair for her to sit, I tuck her into the table before I take a seat. I can't stop staring at her. I can't stop seeing Kennedy sitting across from me. She smiles, and I know this is all right. The pretend is all right for now.

The wine pours smoothly into her glass, and I pour myself one as well. She waits until I've put the first piece of steak into my mouth before she takes a bite.

"We never had room service together. I never bought her flowers. This is something that I have always wanted to do for Kennedy." A confession

154

without judgment by the female sitting across from me. She listens while taking a few sips of the wine.

"Why didn't you?" She searches my face.

"Because I was a stupid little weak wolf."

"Were you a juvenile when you met her?" She's trying to give me an excuse. I have none.

"No, I was full-grown but very stupid." I choose not to look at her, but out the window at the casinos with billboard neon lights that are too harsh for eyes that want to de-focus.

"Aren't we all sometimes?" She takes another drink, no judgment. Nothing but a soft smile that takes away the tension of my shoulders.

"I just wanted to have a nice dinner with her. I wanted to show her I could be a wolf she felt proud of on her arm. I wanted her to love me more." My confession is felt in a tear that drips from the corner of my eye.

Clearing my throat, I say, "Sorry." I wipe my eye before cutting into another piece of steak; she drinks more wine.

"What happened?" Her body leans into the table, a glass of wine held in her hand. No opinion on her face. She seems neutral, safe even.

"I found her, but she was in love with someone else. Someone better than me, stronger than me, someone who gave her everything she needed to reject me. I just wouldn't take no for her answer. So I forced my mark on her in a ceremony that meant nothing at the time. That dress you're wearing is something I think she would have worn at a proper mating ceremony in our pack. You look beautiful in it." The glass of wine does nothing to take away the dryness from my throat, so I put the glass down.

"How long were you mated before she died?"

"Not even a year. My mark faded so fast that I don't even really remember what it looked like." My hand drifts to the spot where nothing remains.

Those eyes stare into mine. "Can I kiss you the way I have always wanted to kiss her?"

Her brows furrow. "You never kissed her?"

"Not the way she should have been kissed by me." I can't face those eyes and have to repeat that this isn't a bad choice before I can pull my head up and look into those eyes again.

"Would you like to dance?" I ask as nicely as I can. I need to move; I can't sit here anymore.

"Of course." She waits for me to pull her chair out and take her hand to help her out. She lets me lead.

"I've never danced with her."

Hazel says nothing back. She just sways with me with her arms around my neck while I close my eyes and inhale. It's now Kennedy that I'm holding; it's Kennedy who is allowing me to lead; it's Kennedy that I feel underneath my palms. Her body moves with mine.

"Can I kiss you?" This is Kennedy I want to kiss...

"Yes," she breathes.

Holding the back of her head in my hand, I tilt her lips to mine. She keeps her eyes open, and I keep mine open as I touch my lips to hers. Gentle, slow, nothing like what we shared before. There are no teeth, no blood, nothing but lips on lips.

Can she taste my tears?

156

Her smell is there through my tears, her smell is there through my sobs, and her smell is there for the pain. Arms hold me through this, and I can taste her tears now.

I taste her scent on skin, I taste her along her neckline, and I smell her scent on hair.

Her chest presses into mine. I can feel the press of her body. My body wants to press itself into her.

"Tell me what you want, Kennedy?"

"I want you, Cash."

Inhaling. Inhaling. Inhaling.

The sound of the zipper pulls down her dress, my hands all over her curves, eyes not leaving her eyes. The dress comes off.

Closing my eyes, letting my tongue taste her. Suck her flesh into my mouth, leaving the impression of teeth across her collarbone.

She gasps. I feel her tremor in my arms.

Picking her up, face to face, I kiss her all the way to the bed with eyes open.

My tongue enters her mouth, and she opens wide for me. She feels soft and light; her chest crushes against my chest. My balls pull up. Fuck, I'm hard.

Inhaling. Inhaling. Inhaling.

I've missed this smell. I've forgotten what she smells like.

Eyes open to eyes.

Kennedy is here with me...

I place her on the bed, face to face. She watches as I take off the suit jacket and climb on top of her on the bed.

She smiles.

I crawl over her body and press my hips to hers.

157

Face to face.

Her fingers start to undo the buttons of my shirt, and I grind into her, feeling Kennedy between my legs. Inhaling, she feels so good. I don't close my eyes. I can't look away from her.

The zipper of my pants pulls down; she inhales as she tugs them down my thighs.

She spreads her legs wider as I settle between them, rubbing against the thinness of her wet underwear.

I inhale as I make my way down her neck to her breasts. Her bra gets taken off, and I get to run my tongue across her nipples. She arches her back and rubs herself against my cock.

Inhaling...

Moving my way down her stomach, to her underwear line, pulling them off. Spreading her legs and letting my tongue work her center. Her hips move up off the bed, and nails are now in my head, anchoring me to her.

Inhaling...

She pulses around my finger, and now I am heavy with a need to be inside her.

Raising up, she spreads her legs wide, and I enter her with a grunt.

Eyes never leaving eyes.

She holds me, wraps herself around me.

I kiss her; she kisses me back, all lips no teeth. No blood.

Pushing in, dragging my cock out, a whimper comes out from my throat as I push back in one last time to explode inside her.

Eyes locking on eyes.

"I love you." I say it like goodbye.

Closing my eyes on her, holding the scent one last time to my nose. She holds me against her. The tears don't stop.

Sobs begin to turn to silence. The tears stop, and finally I can pull my head off her chest.

"I have one request before I leave." It's Hazel I'm looking at. Kennedy's eyes are blurring away.

"What is it?"

"I want you to shave my head."

Hazel smiles with smeared red lips. "Of course I will, Cassius."

Letter 13

Cash,

I'm tired today and you looked tired too— we both are tired. You came in, standing close to the door before you step inside the room. You hesitate. It's like you feel out the mood and either enter or walk away depending on me.

Don't hesitate, Cash. Don't hesitate in your life because of me. You can't.

I've decided I'm not going to fall in love with you. I'm not, because I don't want you to fall in love with me. We're messy enough. We don't need to add love between us. You deserve to be loved, and you deserve to fall in love. Just not with me. I won't give you that memory to hold onto. It's easier for both of us if we keep the love away.

My love has been given to Clayton, and I don't know how to love you in a way you should be. So I'm going to let someone else love you the way it could have been between us. You'll give them love, and they will give you love back. Something special, something just for you and her to share. You're going to need to leave me out of your love. You can't bring me into the relationship because it won't work. So I'm not going to love you. I'm not going to say I love you. I'm not going to let you kiss me. No matter how much I want you to now, I'm not going to give in to what it would feel like to have something gentle against me. I'm too far gone to be saved, and I'm too selfish to give my love of Clayton up for you. I'm no saint and you're no villain. Please try to remember that.

We share a bond, but we don't have love.

Don't be afraid to love. It's beautiful and wonderful. Don't let someone fix you up. Fix yourself up first, then you're ready to be loved again. Don't break someone's heart because you weren't ready to be loved, that's just cruel, and I know you're not cruel.

Kennedy

CHAPTER 14

Regret in Open Letters

The buzz of the hair clipper echoes around the marble walls of the bathroom.

"Are you ready?" Hazel asks. I nod my head, and she starts on the right side of my head. The strip of hair comes off easily, much easier than I thought it would.

"Are you going to take your beard off?" Another strip of hair comes off, falling around the legs of the chair.

"I was thinking about it."

"You should. Fresh face, a new you." She doesn't look at me when she talks. She's focused on taking off the hair, and I think she's enjoying it.

"Have you done this before?"

"I cut Tate's hair at home when he lets me but never buzzed his entire head."

"Is that your boyfriend?" She stops, clipper held in her hand.

"No, Tate's not my boyfriend, but he's more

than a friend. It's hard to explain." She starts on another strip, curling the clipper around the back of my ear.

"Does he know what you do?"

"He knows."

"Does he care?"

"Nope, not really." She takes a sip from the edge of the whiskey glass without making a face at how strong it is to drink it neat. She went through the second bottle of wine while I was showering and asked if I'd like a glass. She poured me one, no ice, straight whiskey. The way it's meant to be sipped, she said.

"I'm not sure I'm going to give to your charity anymore. I don't like how you use the donations." Hazel now judges me.

"You don't have to worry about that. I didn't spend that money. Donations are barely enough to cover the costs to keep the program running. I sell coloring books online and do all graphics and media promotion for the farm."

Hazel kind of laughs out loud. "You sell coloring books?"

"I do. Are you judging what I do for a living?" She stops for a moment and gives me a big smile without any lipstick left on her lips. She points the clippers in the mirror at me with an angle to her head.

"I would never judge a wolf's way of life. If you want to draw coloring books for kids, by all means, do it, but be the best fucking coloring bookmaker you can be." She takes another sip of whiskey. I haven't touched mine. I'm not really a whiskey drinker.

"It's cut-throat out there."

"How do you do?" Hazel finishes what's in her glass.

"I do all right. It's enough."

"Are you in stores?"

"No, just online."

"I know someone who owns this big chain of grocery stores. I could get your product in there for five percent of your sales." Now her smile is shrewd business, a hint of teeth showing.

"You get me into those stores and you're going to take five percent of the profits?"

"Sounds fair." She continues to cut my hair.

"If you can get me into those stores, I'll give you your five percent."

"Deal." The sound comes out crisp.

She doesn't stand too close to me while cutting my hair. My space and her space don't mix. Her robe is secured tight, and I have on my old clothes again.

Our business is over.

Hazel works on the left side now. "You live on a farm?"

"No, well, actually our territory holds a farm on it. It's getting bigger and bigger since Rya came. It started with the bees when she planted this field of wildflowers."

"A field of wildflowers?"

"We didn't question it. She said she needed it, so we planted it. Then the next year, the bees came. They swarmed, so we bought the containers and collected honey. Rya started to give it away as presents to visiting packs or when she went for a visit. Some wolves asked if they could buy more from her, and the next thing that happens is the pack is in the honey business." Hazel stops cutting my hair to listen. She takes my untouched glass and starts to drink from it like it's water.

"After the second year, Rya planted a lot of fruit trees. She wants the pups to be able to climb and pick fruit right from the trees. She started visiting different packs, and some had an animal that they couldn't care for anymore, so we have a pig, Mrs. Oink, and a goat called Mr. Bill."

"Nice names."

"The kids." As if that says everything.

"Rya is the one with the Moon's eyes, right?"

"Yes."

She starts with the top of my head now. Everything is coming off.

"Hazel, thank you."

"You don't have to thank me. You paid me. We had a transaction, nothing more than that. You needed some help with whatever is inside your head, and I was able to do community service and make some money on the side." She takes another sip, longer this time.

"You're going to be all right, Cash."

"You think so?"

"Yeah, I know wolves, and I think you're going to be just fine."

"I feel all right. Not like before her, but I feel all right for the first time in a long time." The hair on my head is now buzzed low; she used a number three setting on me.

"Tommie's a liar. You are worth every penny."

"Tommie does that to show me he cares. If he didn't care, he wouldn't say anything to anyone." Hazel takes a straight razor out of a package.

"I'm not sure. To me, he doesn't seem to like you very much."

Hazel waves her hand in the air. "It's an act."

"I'm not sure. He seems real."

"It's only because I touch his stuff on purpose. I like to get under his skin. It's easy to do, and it's fun to sit back and listen to his threats." She laughs, and it sounds lonely echoing off the walls of the bathroom.

"He threatens you?" My shoulders straighten up.

"He told me he's going to spank me. That's his threat. He's harmless, all teeth no real bite, plus I deserve it a little. I was shit to him when he was younger. He was really small growing up, and he kissed me once, and I laughed at him. I think that had a lasting impression on him, plus now, I take his weed. Tommie and his weed are like some sort of sacred thing." Her eyes are leveled and clear for how much alcohol she's consumed.

"Tommie has some issues. His mate rejected him and is raising the pups of the Alpha as her own and won't leave them to go with Tommie. He's had a rough time with that, plus he's back from school and he really doesn't fit in with the pack. He was picked on a lot when he was younger, really bad, actually. I should have done something, but I didn't."

"Tommie seems like he can take care of himself now."

"He can now, but before…nope. He didn't grow until college, then he came back looking like some model that could kick almost anyone's ass. He has the best weed. Do you smoke?"

"No."

"Too bad. It helps with the edges."

"How long has it been for you?"

"For me?" She stiffens.

"Without your mate."

"Wolf, I don't talk about that." She bristles up, and all her lines become hard and straightened out. It's as if a big *Do Not Disturb* sign hangs from her neck.

There is a pause between us. It lets me know we are strangers.

She watches me shave my face. I really look at myself in the mirror. It's been so long since I've seen me that it takes a few hard minutes to realize this is my face and it's okay to see myself again.

When I'm done, she inspects the finished product. "You're not that bad, Cash. Cleaned up, you aren't that bad at all." She gives me a toothy smile, her eyes lingering everywhere before looking away.

"Thanks."

"I have a ten o'clock tonight, so I need to get ready." She turns on the tap and washes her hands, looks at her teeth.

"Do you like what you do?"

"It's a job that pays the bills. I've met some nice men, some not so nice. They get something, I get something. The end, but sometimes I meet wolves like you who need a wolf like me to make it all right

166

to move on. There's less guilt if you pay for it the first time than actually doing it because you want to fuck someone. Guilt is like a noose. It hangs you after a while."

"I wanted to say goodbye to her."

"Saying goodbye and wanting to fuck someone else is the same thing, isn't it? Do you have someone else you want to fuck, Cash? This is your guilt-free goodbye. You pay me money, and you go back to your pack a new wolf without guilt. I've taken off the noose around your neck. You won't choke on yourself anymore. You've gotten your goodbye, your head's shaved, and right now, I enjoy what I do."

"You're a good wolf, Hazel."

She holds a finger up. "Don't tell anyone. I have an image to maintain." She says her words through that lonely smile that doesn't spread as wide as it could.

We both look at my face in the mirror, silent, inspecting the reflection that's staring back.

"You look good, Cash."

"I feel better." Running my hand over my head, over my clean face, the kids are going to freak out. I can't stop the small laugh that comes out as a breath.

Picking up my bag, standing at the door, we don't hug goodbye after I pay her for her service. She takes the money, and I close the door behind me.

Letter 14

Cash,

We sat on the swing yesterday, gliding back and forth. I think we both wanted to talk, but neither of us could. I have all these words to say to you, but when you're around me, everything seems stuck.

You started talking about the weather, how it's a nice day today. I agreed. Then you moved to food, and I said I wasn't hungry. You told me I looked pretty, and I called you a liar. You said you were trying, and I said stop.

You walked away, and I started to cry because there was nothing more that I wanted to do than sit there with you on the swing and talk about the weather, about food, about how you thought I was pretty.

I wanted to ask you how you thought I was pretty when all I am is ugly to you? How could you look at me and think, she's pretty? It's easier for us if I stay ugly, Cash. It's easier for everyone if I stay this wolf that no one likes that way. In the end, no one will care that I'm gone, even you.

We sacrifice for love, don't we? My sacrifice is staying ugly when all I want to do now is tell you that the weather is good, the food is wonderful, and your face is beautiful. I want to touch your face, I want to feel your lips, I wanted to hold hands with you on that swing. I wanted to ask what attracted you to me. I can tell you I love your back, Cash. You have a nice back, and your arms are strong. Every time you move, I can see your triceps flex: it's a turn-on for me. Arms.

I notice you wear a lot of layers, a lot. Two shirts, a belt, underwear, jeans, even a few rings. You won't get undressed in front of me. You're very private now. Even in front of your family, you have all these layers that you wrap yourself in.

I've made you uncomfortable in your own skin. I'm not even sure you realize it. I do; I realize everything. I'm sorry for that. There is nothing I'd like more than to touch you and tell you how I have this need now to touch your body. I want your hands on me, over me, and when we are in bed together back to back, it takes all my willpower not to turn around and try to hold you.

I was afraid I could never love someone the way I loved Clayton, but Cash, I could have loved you more. If things were different, I could have loved you more.

Kennedy

CHAPTER 15

Letters in the Right Hand

Green eyes meet mine when the door opens.

"You know it's daytime, right?" Clayton states an obvious fact.

"I know."

"Well, come in. I made some soup." He holds the door open wider for me to go in. He hasn't changed the inside of this house since Rya lived here. Everything is exactly the same. There is a single bowl on the table, a spoon placed next to it.

"I see you cut your hair." Clayton doesn't face me. He's getting another bowl from the cupboard and a spoon out of the drawer. He ladles the soup from a pot that's still simmering on the stove.

"I did." I sit down across from him. He places the bowl in front of me.

The package in my hand is placed on the table; this is the last time I touch those letters.

Clayton spoons some soup in his mouth, watching me. I do the same. "This is good soup."

"Everything's from my garden."

"Rya makes a good soup." Once the words are out, Clayton hesitates to swallow what's on his spoon. It's held for a moment longer before he swallows it down, and he starts to stir the broth in the bowl.

"Why are you here, Cash?" Clayton puts his spoon down. Elbows on the table, hands folding like a prayer.

"Do you have anything of Kennedy's left?"

"I told you before, everything of hers was burned. I don't have anything left."

The broth is warm with chunks of soft vegetables in it. I take a few more bites.

"Do you remember Kennedy?"

"What kind of question is that? Of course I remember her. How can I forget her?" His voice is crisp.

"She was afraid you wouldn't remember her." Clayton looks out the window before rubbing at his eyes. It doesn't stop the tears that start to leak out.

"This isn't easy, Cash." Clayton's not looking at me. He's concentrating on the soup bowl.

"She loved you, she didn't love me, and that's not your fault. The minute I came here was the minute you let her go. I shouldn't have blamed you for everything."

Clayton's fingers feel the top of his shaved head, but he doesn't look at me. His shoulders curl around the table. He's still crying, silently.

"We were young. No one could tell us anything. We were the ones that were going to make it. Beat the mate bond." He rubs his hands together before weaving his fingers tight. He breathes out slowly, picking his head up.

"In the beginning, I wanted to keep her for myself. I thought we could fight the bond together. The things I did to keep us together." I see his jaw grind at his back molars. He doesn't look at me but out the window. I can't eat the rest of my soup, so I lay the spoon next to the bowl.

"We hurt a lot of wolves, Kennedy and me. A lot. Now she's gone and I'm left here." He looks around the table. It's empty. Everything inside feels shrine-like empty, hollow even.

"I brought you letters. I wish I could say I didn't read every single one. I did. I wish I didn't." I push the package to the middle of the table. He doesn't move to take them. He just stares with his head down.

"I got the twins, and now you have her letters."

"Thank you, Cash." Again the palms of his hands push into his eyes.

"I need to thank you for your patience with me. I made it difficult for you. I'm sorry about showing up any time I wanted on your territory. You could have killed me. You didn't." My turn to look down at the bowl of soup.

"Your family has been kind to me, too kind. I just couldn't do that to them. Plus there were times that I wanted to go to your pack unannounced and talk with Dallas." His eyes dilate, his nose flares, and his spine straightens.

"Don't do that. Dallas will fucking kill you."

"I'm not afraid of Dallas. I wouldn't do that to Rya. That's why I won't go. Plus it wouldn't change anything. She has a life, a family. It wouldn't change anything." He lets the rest of the air out of his lungs, and his eyes meet mine.

"I'm not going to be coming back here when I leave. I want you to know that. I'm done."

"Good, because there is nothing left for you here. You have everything where you live. This place is only filled with ghosts, nothing more. And ghosts aren't real." Clayton pushes away another tear.

"We were breaking up. That's the sad part. We weren't going to be the ones to make it. What we did, what I did, was for nothing. When Rya came back, I couldn't fight it. The *Wild* wouldn't tolerate Kennedy around him anymore. I loved her, I didn't want to hurt her, but I couldn't fight the bond to Rya. I told Kennedy everything. She didn't understand." Clayton picks up his bowl and mine, putting them in the sink. He stands there with hands clenched around the edges.

"I still love her. I'm sorry, but even after everything, I still love Kennedy, and she won't be forgotten." His edges blur with a few shedding tears that I wipe quickly away. It doesn't hurt as much to hear him say it.

Grief-stricken eyes fall on mine when he turns himself around. Something burns up my throat.

"I could have loved Kennedy more." Clayton stays silent, his lips pressing hard together.

"Do you need anything else, Cash?"

"Nope, I think I'm done here," I reply, standing.

"Good." Clayton goes to the back door and opens it.

A bee flies in, and Clayton is quick to shoo it

back outside. "I have a beehive over there, and they always want to come inside."

I look in the direction he's pointing, and the entire backyard is something even Rya would be impressed with. A garden from a magazine stares back at me.

"You've got a nice garden."

"Thanks, it gives me something to do, and my little sister sells the produce at our stand down the road. It gives her a little extra cash."

There's a pause from him before he lets the screen door close.

"Thanks for bringing the letters."

"They're yours. I just couldn't bring them sooner."

"I understand."

"I always thought you didn't understand, but I know you do."

"I do understand." His voice is rough, dragging up his throat to come out slightly mumbled. He takes a slow breath in.

"I just need to put this all away now. It's time for me to give those letters up."

"Is it easy?"

"Easy?"

"To put it all away."

My stomach twists. "No, it's not easy."

"Uncle Clay." A pup runs with arms spread as fast as he can into the now-open arms of Clayton.

"Max." The pup is tossed high in the air, only to be caught and given a hug with nose nudges into his neck before he puts him down on the ground.

"Where's your mother?"

"Coming." The pup runs to the dock; it looks new.

That island is easy to see from here. It sits solitary, surrounded by water.

"Can we go for a canoe ride, Uncle Clay?"

"Did you eat yet?"

"No."

"Eat first, then we can go." The pup jumps up and runs with his arms pumping into the house.

"Clay, we're all out of tomatoes and onions." Kimberly freezes when she sees me then looks into the house with teeth bared.

"Clayton."

"It's okay, Cash is leaving. He had to drop something off for me."

Kimberly looks weary, fists clenched as if she's ready to fight me again. She's an overprotective little sister who will stand tall with her brother, no matter if she's going to bleed from it.

"Hi, Kimberly." I shove my hands deep in my pockets. No threat. No teeth. No more fighting.

"Hi, Cash." I think this is the first time we have ever said hi to the other.

"Max is getting big." She smiles when I say this. It's not a big smile, just something simple that pulls at her edges.

"He is." She's still wary but has settled her ridge fur down.

"So what's going on? You guys are friends now?" She looks at Clayton and me.

"No," both of us say at the same time.

"I won't be back. I just wanted to drop off something and I'm gone." I can tell her eyes don't believe me.

"Goodbye." I turn toward Clayton.

"Bye, Cash."

We don't hug; we don't shake hands. I just turn and walk away with a promise not to come back here. Ever.

Letter 15

Dear Clayton,

I don't know how many times I start this and stopped. Nothing seems right. I don't know where to begin. So I want to begin with I love you.

I've always loved you. Only you. No one else.

I painted a picture of our island, how I remember it. I want you to have it.

That was the best time of my life. I'm not sure anything can compare to that spot, that place, who we were there.

The first time we went there alone was when we were eight and made a fort in the pines. Do you remember that? We had a fire and pretended that's where we lived. When we were older, it became our refuge from the world, our parents, on that island. That's the first place we kissed; it's the first place we gave ourselves to each other.

I've been remembering so much about that

island. It was ours; no one can take that time away from us. No one.

I feel as if I am sinking, drowning, and all that I can hold onto now is the memory of our island. I feel guilty having his pups inside me and not ours.

I feel guilty for wanting him and that you are becoming a memory on an island that I can't stop thinking about. This is so screwed up, but I know what you were talking about now about the bond. It's hard to look away even when you want to. It's hard to fight against it.

Our love was never meant to leave bite marks and bruises in other wolves' skin, but it did, didn't it? I was selfish, Clayton. So very very selfish to try and keep your love all to myself.

I thought by having Kimberly have a pup that our love would stay just between you and me. I was wrong about that. So very wrong. You told me pups weren't important to you, and I cried and told you how important they were to me. I put your sister in danger and that wasn't love, was it?

In the end, our love hurts everyone, including ourselves.

I'm dying, Clayton. I can feel myself every

day slipping away. I'm tired and don't want to fight anymore. I don't want to do anything but close my eyes and rest for a while. You might think it's selfish that the twins will grow up without a mother, but I think it's selfless to give them a chance in this life without someone like me. My love is poison. It made me do things I never thought I'd do for love.

You tried to tell me about the bond, but I wouldn't listen to you. I thought you could fight harder against it; I thought you were stronger. I had faith in you, and you tried to tell me, but I was selfish because I couldn't let you go.

I knew you loved me, and now I know what you went through. I love you, Clayton, but I can't stop thinking about Cash. I can't stop wanting to feel him or have him feel me, but I love you. Now I understand it all. All those years you had to fight against something as natural as breathing for me, for us. And in the end, I understand it all, and it makes me love you even more.

You tried so hard and I never understood that fight.

I've stopped dreaming about you. It's been months now, but I can't get our island out of my head. If I could go back in time, would I do it all over again? Maybe.

It feels as if I'm being swallowed down by something rotten. I feel as if I stink of rot and leave ruin in my wake. This family tolerates me, but they don't love me, and I don't blame them at all. I'm a stranger here; I refuse to make myself anything more than that. Why? Because it's easier that way for everyone. It's easier to move on from a stranger than a friend.

Caleb called and said that Rya left your pack today to go her own way, and I know that you have fallen in love with her. I knew it as soon as I heard that you let her go. You let me go, and now you let her go.

Don't feel guilty for loving her. It can't be helped. You fought too long.

I'm going to be nothing more than a memory that will fade in time, and you are going on with your life. I'll only be remembered in pieces, in bits of things, and it kills me inside, because in the most selfish way possible, I want you to remember me on our island together. That's the person I want you to remember. That's how I want to be remembered by you, on our island free of the world, while we played in our own world.

When I think of you, I think of our island now—those were the best days of my life.

You gave me my best days.

I love you, Clayton, and I'm selfish because I can't let you go. I don't know, maybe it's different for females; we might have a harder time letting things go, letting our love go?

When you finally had the real talk with me underneath the apple tree, I was on my knees begging you not to do this, to fight harder. I was begging you not to do this to us. You broke my heart that day. I knew it was coming. I knew it, even before Rya showed back up in the pack. It was going down that path. I didn't want to see our end. I tried stopping the inevitable. I tried stalling the end of us. That was wrong. I just couldn't let you go. I wasn't ready for the breakup. I wasn't ready not to have you in my life anymore. I wasn't ready to be alone without you. You've always been there; I don't remember a time you weren't there. We always walked side by side, even as pups. We were a team, and I wasn't ready for all of it to end.

Now my end is coming near, and I feel prepared. In a strange way, I'm calm. I can handle death, but I couldn't handle losing you.

CASSIUS

I'm afraid you're going to be able to handle losing me, and it kills me inside, but I understand it. You already gave me up without any kind of fight. I'm sure you're finding a way to finally breathe again. I know I was choking you in the end, and now the noose around your neck is gone.

Breathe, breathe, breathe.

Love, Kennedy

CHAPTER 16

Hands are Meant to Feel

It starts with Cassius entering the house, and everyone goes quiet. Even the twins stop running toward him. He's shadowed to me, a big blur that isn't in focus.

It ends with Caleb saying, "Brother," and embracing him in a long hug.

"I didn't recognize you at first."

"I didn't, either," Cassius says back to him.

"Hey, it's your dad." The shadow of Cassius bends down, and the twins are reluctant to get closer. Dee moves faster than Ken, who still holds an exaggerated limp.

"What happened to your knee?" There's a lowered tone of concern to Cassius.

"The goose got him, but killer, over there, got the goose," Caleb answers because the twins aren't making a sound.

"Specs, you killed the goose?" He sounds surprised.

182

"The *Wild* murdered it. Only the feathers are left," Caleb growls low in his throat.

"I've always hated that goose, it was too aggressive around the kids, but Rya insisted she needed a guardian for the chickens."

"I can't believe you killed that goose." Cassius seems shocked by the news.

"Feel my face. It's me, Dee." I can see a blur of movement as the twins get closer. "See? It's your dad, just without hair. Like Ken."

I pause, feeling the beat of my heart in my throat. Each beat pulsing harder, faster, my ears fill with the sound of rushing blood. He's shaved his head. How I wish I could see him right now. See what he looks like without the layers of hair that hide his face.

"Specs, where's your glasses?"

There is a pause, and I open my mouth, but words are trapped like spit under my tongue that gets swallowed down with a now-closed mouth.

"Battle wounded, the frame broke." Caleb uses his voice.

"Specs' *Wild* killed the goose," Ken says really loud.

"Did she? Well, the goose had it coming. Let me see your knee." Cassius seems to kneel down on the floor while Ken gets closer, limps harder now.

"His leg isn't broken. Dallas said it's normal for kids that age to limp around for a little while after the injury takes place."

"That's a cool Band-Aid." I hear Cassius place a kiss to Ken's knee.

"How was Vegas?"

"I'll tell you later..." Cassius pauses. "Thanks for watching them. Are you guys ready to go home? I'm tired." Cassius pulls up to his full height. I stand. All of our stuff is at the door.

"Clayton said you came by and dropped off some letters for him."

"That's the last time I go there, Caleb. It's the last time going there."

"I believe you this time."

He helps Ken get on his shoes, and Dee does it herself. She's more independent. Once she knows how to do something, she won't allow anyone else to do it for her.

"You have everything?" Cassius seems to be speaking to me, so I nod yes.

The kids run toward his truck, and I get to hold onto Cassius's shirt. He's slow leading the way to the truck, mentioning a dip in the driveway, to be careful. He opens the door, and before I get in, he fixes the strap of my dress that's fallen past my shoulder. His finger slides up slowly, almost deliberately slow. His hand raises up to my neck until he curls a piece of hair around my ear before pulling his fingers quickly away. He clears his throat.

He has leaned in. I can almost feel his chest against mine. "New dress?" He takes my bags out of my hands, not saying another word. He shuts the door as soon as I'm seated. I can hear him buckle up the kids' car seats.

"How was your trip, Daddy?"

"Good. How was your sleepover with Uncle Caleb? What did you do?"

184

Dee talks the entire time; Ken doesn't say much. She tells him about the murder of the goose, about how Ken needed two Band-Aids for his boo-boo, and about me sleeping in my big girl bed.

I want to say if he can change, I should too. I don't, and I feel a hand on my shoulder with a squeeze of flesh before those fingers fall away. I can still feel the warmth of his palm as we pull into the driveway.

"You slept in your own bed, Specs?"

I keep looking forward, not at him, and nod my head yes.

"Wow, we have a lot to talk about tonight." I can't tell him that I woke up all night long with pressure around my neck and the screams of *him* in my ear.

When he parks the truck, the kids get out first. He carries all the bags, and I walk a little behind him.

It's quiet when we get inside. I wish I could see their faces. I know they are both hugging him to them. I can hear a muffled cry with a lot of throat clearing.

"We have a lot to talk about, Cash." Luna Grace talks low, and I head upstairs. It's family time, and I'm not going to intrude on what they want to ask Cassius in private.

Letter 16

Dear Clayton,

You were the wolf I loved, you were the only one that I ever wanted, and I think it ate me alive. Everything consumed me, and I wanted to keep everything to myself. I think that's where it all went wrong.

I got selfish, greedy, and didn't want to let you go when we should have let each other go.

I refused to hear anything anyone was saying. I refused to see the way my friends started to leave me when they met their mates. I refused to listen to them. I refused to listen to anyone because I knew deep down they were right. I just refused to listen because our love was real; we were the ones that were going to make it to the very end. I sacrificed for loving you, I knew we couldn't have our own children, and I told myself that was all right. I told myself our love was enough for me.

You were worth all my sacrifice.

Now, I'm pregnant with twins from my mate, and all I want to think about is you. It's so hard to let you go.

Cash gave me a choice. He said that if I want to, I could go back to you. He told me that he would let me go, but he keeps the kids. He's giving me an out. I think it's more so I start trying to live, to fight harder to stay alive. I think he's trying to goal set for me.

I'm not going to survive the birth. I already know. My Wild died inside me; she's gone.

186

There is nothing but this ever-extending hollowness in my chest.

Given the choice, I would pick staying with Cash than going back to you.

A little each day I'm able to connect the pieces my love for you has left me in. It was small at first, like waking up without crying because I was without you. I could eat things without everything reminding me of you. Tastes, smells, sounds aren't as triggering as they once were.

I used to hate sunsets because we always spent them together. It was hard to get over the sunsets. I painted a mural in the twins' room; there's a small space dedicated to you. It's us holding hands with our faces toward the setting sun. Only our backs are seen, and it's like we are walking hand in hand into the water, together forever. It's a picture full of lies because that won't ever happen, but it's a picture of a fairytale, my fairytale ending for us.

I'm letting you go, Clayton. I'm letting everything go, and it feels all right now.

Soon for you it will be a year, then it will turn into two, three, four years, and my hope is that you are happy, that I'm remembered with love and a smile on your face, not with tears coming down your face and acid crawling up your throat.

I don't want to be that ghost ache in your gut.

Where your skin like a wolf not like a skin that's turned into a ghost. I know you, Clayton, I know you better than I know myself, and you're going to blame him for a lot of things, but it's not only Cash's fault what happened to me. I take credit for everything as well.

Don't kill him when he comes for you, because he will come for you. I know it down to my bones. He's going to try, and I want you to be patient with him. He has my children to raise, and I need him alive.

This is so hard for me, but you have to go find Rya. I know you let her leave because you were in love with her. Don't feel guilty for that. Don't feel guilty for falling in love with someone else that isn't me. I know I was the one that kept you from her. Don't let yourself keep her from you. Go find her and start a life with her. It's going to be hard for her to forgive you, but she forgave me, and that says a lot. You've got the bond; use it.

I'm sorry I still love you, but I'm starting to love him more, and in the end, I want you to be happy. At the end of all of this, I want you to be happy.

I love you, Clayton, as my first love, as my best friend.

This is me trying to say goodbye to you.

Love, Kennedy

CHAPTER 17

Feel the Flush of Red

A knock sounds on the door before it's open. "You're still up?"

Clinging wet hair has Cassius turning around with his back facing me.

"Sorry, Treajure. I thought you'd be dressed by now."

I pull one of his shirts on quickly before really being dry; my underwear slips up fast before he turns himself around. I think his breathing has stopped because I can't hear anything. No sound, just a blur in the room without noise.

I sit on the bed, fingers curling into the covers. The sheets feel new and untouched.

Cassius clears his throat, all quiet, that trails a quick swallow. "Where are your glasses? I'll fix them." I touch the bedside table drawer. He comes into the room, closing the door behind him. I don't think the two of us have ever been in this room together. It was Dallas's old room, the only one up here with its own bathroom. Luna Grace said a female has to have her own bathroom, and Cassius moved into his old room. They all thought it would work, a new room, a new bed, new paint on the walls. Nothing worked, and now here I am sitting on the bed with that weight starting around my neck.

When I reach to open the drawer, he stops me with a light touch. "I'll get them." I can hear his small toolbox open; he places it right beside me. Somehow he's kneeling now in front of me, not standing.

"This screw always gives me trouble, Specs. No matter how much I keep adjusting it, somehow it always adjusts itself back out." The steam of his breath brushes against the fine hairs on my temples.

He edges himself a little closer; my knees push out to either side of his hips.

"That was a brave thing you did, taking on a guardian goose. Ken told me you saved his life. He told me everything." He's a blur even this close, even with his chin almost touching my forehead.

"Thank you, Treajure." He leans forward, whispering it like smoke in my ear. I swallow too loud; I can hear it in my ears. My insides tighten— thighs tense.

The *Wild* whines inside.

Skin is a great source of pain, but right now, it's the greatest source of pleasure.

Cassius scoots himself closer, looming, protective, and my legs spread wider.

"The frame's still good. It's the screws that are worth nothing. I'll order you another frame tomorrow. I think you got a lemon here, Specs." I swear I feel something electric between us. The hairs on my arms are standing on end; I can feel my skin rise up with goosebumps. It takes everything not to shake my spine out.

"You have long eyelashes." His finger sweeps over one eye, then the other. Tiny catches of pleasure prickle across my flesh.

He strokes the outside of my ears, taking all the clinging hair away from the front of me to the back. My nipples feel exposed now. I'm afraid if he's looking down he'll see them rubbed up against the damp cotton material.

"You've got nice hair. It's thick." I can tell his chest is rising with how deep he is breathing.

My inner thighs accommodate the width of him, spreading so he's now so close that I think our chests could touch. He'd be able to feel the hardness of my nipples if he just leaned in a little closer.

The *Wild* within whines low.

He continues to fix the glasses, taking his time, and when he turns to place something on the table, his forearm brushes against my chest; nipples scrape the damp material of his shirt. I stiffen up, clench internally.

My cheeks feel too hot. The ceiling fan does nothing to cool the room down.

"Almost done." I have to catch myself not to whimper a puppy pout of a sound.

His fingers touch the side of my face while putting on my glasses. The soles of my feet press into the carpet, toes curling as if to try and hold me still.

"Perfect." He says it as if it pains him.

Before I can look at his face, he peels a layer off his body. There's something about watching him take one of his shirts off. The way he grabs the collar from behind his head and pulls up and off.

"It's hot in here." I notice it's stifling hot; the wet hair clings to the back of my shirt. He has a fine layer of shine to his neck and face.

Our eyes meet.

"What do you think?" He strokes the outside of my ear, one of his hands on my bare thigh. It's heavy, weighty, and warm.

He looks slightly uncomfortable as our eyes lock on each other's. "Say something." The sound of him has dropped low and is full of breath. He chews on his lower lip, dragging it inside his mouth.

It takes a while to uncurl my hand from the bedspread, to raise up and touch the side of his face. A sound cracks through his throat, low with a rumbling range.

The pads of my fingers feel down his smooth jawline, the first time I've seen him without a full beard. I let my finger slide underneath his lower lip, feeling how he fits together. His mouth is barely open; he's breathing through his nose.

His eyes appear sharper, trained on my face.

My hands feel his hair that's cut close to his scalp. I lift up slightly to feel the back of his head with my hands; our cheeks get close to the other's.

His hand climbs up my thigh, resting where his shirt ends. Blunt nails run back down my thigh, back up as the material of his shirt inches upwards. There's something primal that comes through his shirt to press into my chest.

My insides clench deeper, and a small sound escapes out of my throat.

I watch this male's eyes, hungry. His pupils are dilated, the black growing darker, nose flared, and he looks about to shift through his skin.

The soft seam of his lips brushes across my cheek. "I'm not good at this, Treajure." Words press against my ear; no one but us could hear him right now.

He drags his cheek across mine before pulling away. He stands to smooth down his shirt. Cassius plays with his face as if he still has a wild beard.

"Goodnight, Specs." He opens and closes the door before I even have time to catch my breath. My heart's in my throat, and I have this unexplained pressure deep down between my legs.

I'm not sure I can sleep now for want of touching him, and I can't stop wondering if he's going to touch himself like I am right now, thinking about him.

Letter 17

Cash,

When the kids are ready, when you are ready, paint the room. Start fresh.

The painting was there only for you to tell stories to the children as they grew, but when they are done with the room they share together, when they get too big, paint over the room. Let them move on; let yourself move on.

You don't need the painting anymore.

I'm putting that picture up of Clayton and me so you have something to focus on. I want it to burn at your gut because I love him more, and in the end, it's his hand I want to hold on my way to the Moon, not yours.

When it doesn't burn at your gut anymore to look at it, you are ready for someone else. You've let me go, and that's all I really want. You deserve to share love and be loved in a way that I could never give you or want to give you.

Remember, I will always choose him, not you.

Kennedy

CHAPTER 18

Red Swirls of Emotions

The sound of the shower wakes me. The sun isn't even up yet as I slide out from underneath the bed with shame clinging to the bones of my spine. Tonight, I'll try again. I need to change.

My room is dark, and so is the bathroom, but the door is cracked slightly, and I can make out Cassius just enough through the shadowed glass to see the hard outline of his body.

This isn't appropriate, but this is the first time I've seen Cassius completely stripped out of all the layers he usually wears. I've seen males walk around without clothes, I've seen males after their shift, but this.

Cassius is just more…

Soap is being lathered between his hands. I can see the movement of him cleaning his neck, his chest, working along the line of his torso. More soap is lathered. He bends, cleaning his thighs and lower legs. He runs his hands up his thighs again

196

and stops in an area that holds the maleness of his scent. A rush of breath is pulled in from his mouth just underneath the noise of the shower. My breath also becomes a quiet race out.

Narrowing my eyes, I try to bring more of him into focus from the shadow of the glass shower. If he were to come out, I'd be standing here, guilty of spying on him. What would he say to me? I should leave, crawl back underneath the bed, but I don't leave my spot; in fact, I creep up a few inches closer. I want to make more of him out, not just the outline of movement.

This isn't right, yet I make no effort to move.

Another low moan just below the fall of water, his one hand is pressed against the tile. Warm water is felt coming out of the room like a summer breath on my skin.

What would he say if I joined him? Open the shower door, catch him with his hand around his cock? Would he stop what he's doing? Would he touch me? What would happen if I slide the glass back and step in?

The water keeps pouring, and I keep standing here, unable to move. A heat spreads below my mound; a slickness starts. I feel myself growing slick with the way his low sounds barely make it out from underneath the spray of the showerhead.

A part of me wishes I'd be caught by him. Another part would be mortified.

He never notices me when I want him with my ruby earrings in. He only notices when I struggle with training or when I'm a sweaty mess from pulling weeds in the garden. When that stupid goose chased me through the yard and he yelled for me to get him. He never notices the important parts, the red parts of me that showed him I was available. He never noticed those times I gathered my hair up at the top of my head to expose those earrings; he never even glanced in the direction of me. Never.

I want to touch myself the way he's touching himself right now. I can hear his breathing becoming lower, his body shifting, another quiet noise from his throat. His shoulders curl, head angled down.

The space between my thighs is warmer now, the slickness pressed into the cotton of my underwear. My nipples are sensitive, and I reach up to squeeze one of my breasts that barely fit in my hand, wishing it was his big hand that palmed me through his t-shirt. Thighs can't handle the weight of all this; they shake now.

A whimper escapes through the sound of the water. His body stills, no more movement before the now coldness of the shower hits me in the face; he's turned it on to freezing cold. The water stops, and I back up into his room, slip underneath the bed, and hold my breath until he dresses and leaves as quietly as he can.

The minutes are counted, one, two, three... I make it to ten before I come out, dash for my room, and look in the shower, imagining I was in there with him. I'm on edge, ready to explode. The coldness of the room does nothing to stop the fire in my belly from growing.

Something is wrong with me. All I can think about is Cassius as I lay on my bed, feeling the flat line of my belly, squeezing my thighs together tight. I ache.

My hand almost feels soothing pressed against the material of my underwear before dipping underneath the band, sliding down my smooth mound. I imagine myself stepping into that shower, him with those surprised eyes. His hand now replaces my hand; it's his fingers lazily rounding against my sex. I'm spurred on with the blurred display through the shower glass of his outlined body, the way his throat made those sounds that were barely loud enough to hear.

Sunrise is starting to peek through the open blinds.

Working myself harder, faster, pressing my teeth into my bottom lip from making any noise, I feel desperate, sweaty, too hot for the t-shirt that's clinging to my skin now.

There's different energy now from seeing Cassius doing that, something more concrete to concentrate on while my slick fingers work myself up into something that provides a few seconds of mind-numbing bliss. Everything is forgotten when I search for this release; nothing else matters but this, right now. This overpowering feeling that takes over my entire surface and insides.

Opening my legs wider, pretending it's him I'm opening up for, not my own hand.

A helpless moan comes out from my throat, breathing heavier, the sinking feeling of my spine pressed against the mattress, thighs are trembling now, toes gathering the material of bedspread up, holding on tight as my pulse races up my throat, another moan, hard this time, a sound louder than I thought possible coming out of my throat.

His name in my head on repeat over and over again, eyes squeezing shut.

Another moan out and the click of the door knob before it opens.

I freeze, eyes still closed.

"Treajure, are you all right?"

My heart's pounding…oh no… Quickly, I take my hand out from between my legs.

Opening my eyes, I have to blink again just to make sure he's really standing there with this shocked expression on his face.

"I thought something was wrong."

My legs close quickly. His eyes pull up to mine but look away, quickly.

"I heard a noise—" He almost stutters the words out.

I can't move, and he's trying not to acknowledge what he's just seen. His eyes are going everywhere but to mine. They fall on the slickness of my fingers. He inhales, looks away quickly, and I am frozen in my spot.

"I thought something was wrong." He steps out of the room. My gut wants to spill around me, and I have to concentrate on not letting my bowels get the best of me.

"I'm sorry." He closes the door, and all I want to do is crawl underneath the bed and hide for the rest of my life.

Letter 18

Cash,

Tell your mother and father thank you. They have hearts of the Moon. It wasn't easy for them to keep loving me when I never gave them much of anything back. I heard your father explain to you once that we only learn from the hard things in life. Watch her, learn from her, think before you act. He was giving you advice, but you were making excuses for everything he said; you weren't ready to listen to him. You were only ready to keep punishing yourself. You need to stop and start learning to love yourself again.

Love yourself.

Nothing good comes from hating yourself. The past is gone. It won't come back to us no matter how much we want to change things. Nothing will bring back the past, but what we can do, what you can do, is start by loving yourself again.

Start with the little things by looking at yourself in the mirror and not just hanging your head while you brush your teeth. Look at your eyes. You have beautiful blue eyes.

Start by listening to music again, you loved music, but now it only hurts your heart and you can't bear to listen to anything that makes you happy.

Start with a song and let it stay on until it ends without shutting off the radio. Let the songs finish, and soon you might even start to hum along to them.

Start by buying yourself something new—a shirt, jeans, shoes, something that's a little too much money—but understand you're worth the splurge.

Start by talking with someone. Let your feelings out, Cash. You need to get those knotted-up feelings out and in the open so someone can help you the way you need to be helped. Talk about your feelings.

Start by playing games again. You and your brothers used to play a lot of games. Start with playing again. Start winning again, start losing again, just start playing.

Start by living, not staying dead inside. You get to live. Don't regret not living a life meant for you because no one can live your life. It's yours. Own it. Love it.

Start with the sun on your face.

Start with rain on your face.

Start with a clear conscience. I didn't want to live. That's the truth. I'm scared to die, scared to live. I've given up, and it's settled me now.

I'm calm.

Be calm, Cash.
Kennedy

CHAPTER 19

Emotions Cling on Soft Lips

It's mid-afternoon when Cassius calls me into my room.

"The other night and the next day," he whispers, "it was inappropriate. I'll try not to let it happen again. It got ahead of me again." Cassius seems uncomfortable and shifts around on his feet, his eyes trained on my ears. He walks out without anything more to say. It's been the most he's said to me in the last two weeks besides awkward thank yous and "do you want something, Treajure?" before he turns his back to face the wall while I slip underneath his bed in the middle of the night when the weight around my neck makes it unbearable to breathe anymore.

Every night is a fight to stay on top of the bed, and every night is a failure when I slide underneath his bed, promising myself I'll stay in my bed tomorrow.

Everything becomes all noise and growls

downstairs, a commotion of hard stomps on wood floors.

"Cash, back up," Alpha Clinton demands as his body fills the space of the front door.

"I'm not going to do anything." There is a measure to Cassius's word; they feel real this time. Different from the last time when Clayton showed up to go into the Wilds of Valentine, he challenged his father's decision about letting Clayton eat. It's not his pack, it's not his right to do that, and Alpha Clinton told him it's the right thing to do. We will always do the right thing no matter how hard it might be. The look Cassius gave his father felt like a deep betrayal; it pushed his father back slightly, and his mother had to come to her mate's side and tell her son that right now it hurts, but in time you'll understand that it's the right thing to help those weaker and suffering. His mother also told him that it was her decision to allow Clayton to go to the Wilds and not his father's. So if you are mad at someone, be mad at me. Her chin went up, waiting for Cassius to say something.

He didn't.

Cassius moves away to stand in front of the big bay window, creeping toward him until I'm slightly behind him but can see outside.

Clayton gets out of the SUV and looks around, inhaling. It's hard to hold the grimace in when Hazel gets out from the passenger side. She's dressed in a small t-shirt, jeans, and flip-flops. Her hair falls past her shoulders, and she's wearing sunglasses.

Caleb gets out from his minivan, and Tommie

jumps out, opening the side door for Addie.

"That's Clayton's new Beta?" Alpha Clinton asks Dallas, who is trying to muscle his way around his father, who is stuck in the frame.

"Dallas, settle down." His father shoves an elbow underneath the ribs of his son.

"You knew he was coming. This shouldn't be a shock." The Alpha's voice is controlled, but there is a huff of breath out when his son tries again to muscle the jam of his father from the door frame. He moves him to the side but barely.

"Not in the house." Luna Grace now comes from the other end of the house. Alpha Clinton settles tight muscles down, and Dallas seems to stop flexing.

There's not a crack of white in the blue sky when we all step outside. The sun's harsh, and I can't stop squinting while looking at the wolves milling around until Luna Grace and Alpha Clinton greet them formally.

Clayton's got a stiff back as Dallas approaches behind his father.

"It's nice to see you again." Luna Grace greets Clayton first.

"Thank you for having us, and thank you for allowing Tommie to come here and be given a chance to let his *Wild* out." Clayton is serious and extremely polite. He wears his hair like the available males of the Valentine Pack do. He's nothing like he is when he has to handle Cassius.

"Not a problem." Alpha Clinton's voice has the visitors not moving forward. They all stay where they are, inspecting the big silverback male, who has a dusting of grey at his temples—he's holds a commanding shape.

"Welcome to the Valentine Pack." The Luna looks on at the rest of them.

"This is Tommie. He's my new Beta." Tommie wears his hair short, cut to his scalp, and he's as big as Caleb.

"This is Hazel and Addie. They've decided to join the pack."

The Alpha nods his head to each of them. The Luna goes to Hazel. "Nice to meet you, Hazel." There is a quick press of cheek together. Hazel keeps her chin raised, shoulders even; there is a swing to her cherry drop earrings.

"Addie, nice to meet you." Addie's cheek presses to her. She doesn't meet Luna's eyes, and her shoulders do curve around slightly.

"I've brought you some fruit wine." She hands the Luna the gift, and a smile stretches wide across her face.

"Thank you, I've never had fruit wine before."

"Tommie, enjoy yourself out there and let your *Wild* lead you."

"Thank you, Luna." Tommie gives a small nod, head bowed, cheeks flush.

"We were going to have a barbecue tonight. Would you like to stay?" The Luna offers, and I can see the bristle along Dallas's spine.

Clayton and Dallas are both looking at each other. "Thank you, but we need to get back. We wanted to see Tommie off." Clayton looks down the driveway when Ken and Dee come running toward their father, and Chance follows behind them toward his father with arms outstretched.

Cassius picks both of them up and nudges at their cheeks before putting them down.

"They look like her." Clayton moves toward the twins, but Cassius becomes all teeth.

A warning growl pushes through his chest, and Clayton stops, drops his hand. "Sorry." An apology that I never heard come from Clayton before.

Chance points his finger at Clayton. "Who's that?" No one answers him.

The look in Clayton's eyes could make me cry mercy for him. All these times I've seen him, I never knew how much devastation he held inside him. I knew he was hurting, but I never thought he was in pieces.

"We need to go." Clayton turns toward the two females, but his entire body freezes. Coming down the driveway is Rya in a light flowered dress. She's nothing but flowing hair and pregnant belly.

Clayton holds his hands behind his back, and nothing breathes excepts for Clayton. There is a soft flush that holds to the back of his neck.

"Clayton." Rya acknowledges him first.

It takes a few moments before I can see movement from Clayton's chest.

"Rya." One word sounds of thick sorrow, hard pain.

Rya's not smiling—neither is Dallas.

"We were going." Clayton backs himself away, creating a giant space. "I just came here to drop off Tommie." His voice sounds faster than normal; usually with Cassius, he has a slow drawl.

"I—" He pauses, a hard blink from Clayton—his

pieces are falling around him. "I'm happy for you, Rya."

Clayton turns his back on them before any more can be said and walks toward his car. Hazel comes up beside him.

"Are you all right?" Hazel questions.

"I'm fine." The door shuts, and Clayton is gripping the steering wheel, tight, with white knuckles before he turns it on.

Addie and Hazel both hug Tommie before getting inside with Clayton.

They pull away—it's quiet until Caleb opens his mouth. "Barbecue?"

Dallas and Rya walk into the house holding hands. Cassius is already inside with the twins.

Tommie passes by with a backpack slung over his shoulder. "Hi, Treajure."

It makes me smile. He's remembered my name.

They sit around the table and talk with Tommie. The pups are wild and showing off for the newcomer. I take Chance and the twins outside when more wolves show up at the house for the gathering. Friday evening bean bag toss and sippers to whoever can make it after work.

Warm sand slips through my fingers in the sandbox. The kids are playing with their dump trucks, and more little ones join them. It's not only a gathering for the adults and juveniles, but for the pups as well.

Dee's burying my feet underneath a mountain of sand.

I'm watching Cassius, who is sitting in a lounge chair drawing in his book. There's no more beard on his face, and it's hard to get used to looking at his neck, all exposed as if waiting for something to happen.

The summer heat gets under my skin. My entire body feels flushed, overwhelmed with warmth.

"Specs, you want to play?" Cassius calls. He's now standing next to one of the boards for the bean bag toss. His face glistens in the sun, he's wearing a few shirts, but I notice he's not wearing the ring anymore. His hand seems naked without it.

Pulling my feet out from where they were buried, I keep my shoes off. The grass feels cool underneath the soles of my feet. He has no shoes on his feet; his toes are painted purple.

"You're not going to win this time. This is my day," he teases when he tosses me my bags for the game.

We stare at each other from the opposite ends of the yard. "Females first."

I remember the first time he coaxed me to play. There were so many wolves and overwhelming sounds that I couldn't stop shaking. I lost the first game, and the second one, but after a while, the noise was something that was held in the background because all that I could concentrate on was Cassius and the edge of his smile every time I sank a bag in the hole. It was our first high five, hand slapping hand, and I didn't wash my skin that night. It was my secret to smell Cassius's scent that clung to my hand underneath his bed. He asked me if I was catching a cold because I was breathing too hard. It wasn't normal, he said, and had Dallas check me out at the clinic in the morning.

He blinks when I push the hair that's stuck to my neck. It feels damp when I tie it up but a lot cooler having it off my back.

When some females walk by, they say hi to the both of us, but they treat Cassius different now. They go into his space, and some even put a hand on his hip or touch his head. I don't like it, and at times I have to stop the *Wild* from intervening. She wants to claim him as her territory; she doesn't like those that trespass.

Cassius smirks when he lands the first point, and my smirk is just as keen when I land a point.

"You think you're going to beat me, Specs?" My body bends to that voice, that shuffle of sound. I'm terrified that he'll notice, he'll see right through me and know how much I want him.

The music is turned up, a favorite song of Rya's. She's dancing in the grass with Dallas, who holds her as close as her pregnant belly will allow.

"Nice shot." A compliment that makes the *Wild* strut in my skin.

"Did you see that, Specs? I'm coming for you. It's my time. Winning time." He heckles me through a crooked smirk.

The party blurs, and it's only Cassius and me. The sweat drips down my back; I can feel it run down between my chest. The sun is starting to set.

Cassius at times will sway to the music, and it's the first time I've seen him this loose, not as tied into himself. He catches me staring—I'm unashamed.

My heart hammers. I've had a gap in reality.

He looks away.

I can taste blood from the bite down on my tongue.

The next three throws he misses, and I sink all of mine. He looks uncomfortable now.

The party is full-on, most of the pack is here, and when I win the game, he gives me my prize in the form of a high-five and, "Good game." When he sits down at an empty picnic table, a few females sit with him, with full plates. They start talking with red lipstick smiles.

This is what it feels like to drown, to suffocate on the last breath.

Caleb is at a table with Tommie and Carson, who are sitting close to each other. I take a seat beside Caleb, not wanting to leave the party, but not wanting to stand by myself watching Cassius being fawned over by the reds of the pack.

"Do you mind if I sleep over tonight, Caleb?" Carson can't stop the blush on his face as he asks. Tommie rubs at his head as if he has hair there.

"What do I look like, some sort of bed and breakfast?" Tommie leans back from the table. He isn't used to Caleb, but Carson is ready for him.

"I'll put twenty-five on the counter when I leave." Carson sips his beer, but his eyes keep falling on Tommie.

"You need to do the dishes. I'm not your domestic."

"Done." Carson is quick with that word.

"Does anyone need another?" Tommie stands with an empty bottle in his hand.

Caleb's eyes squint at him. "Nice line."

"Your brother introduced me to that line. I like it,

a lot."

"Of course he did. It was my line before he stole it. Right, Carson?"

"Well, it looks like you aren't using them anymore, so…" His brother shrugs his shoulder. Caleb has this pout that looks puppyish on a full-grown male.

"Treajure, you want one?" I'm a little shocked Tommie touched my shoulder when he asked.

"Get her a whiskey vodka. She does well on them." I shake my head no. Caleb laughs. It's been a big joke, and for a long time he called me the puker. His mother told him to stop and he told his mother it's only because he loves me that he teases me like a sister. I felt bad for shanking him the next day, but he had it coming.

"She'll take water, thanks. I'll take a beer." There's something violent in the way Cassius is looking at Tommie.

"Push over." Cassius sits down and places a plate of food between us.

Everything seems to get quiet.

"Treajure, Crane's having a party tonight. You should come with us." Carson and Caleb both eye Cassius.

A half not so funny laugh, a pause, then, "No, she's not going to that kind of party."

Caleb snickers, and I can see how it clings underneath of Cassius's skin.

"I got us some food."

We are sitting side by side, close enough for our thighs to touch. I'm still. Not moving even to eat.

"Open your mouth." Cassius's voice is low, and

213

his brothers blatantly stare.

"What? She has a habit of not eating." He talks to them as if it makes perfect sense. I've never been hand-fed by him before.

I take a piece of warm steak from his fork and swallow it down before he holds out the fork for me to take. Both of us start to eat off of one plate, and his brothers haven't said a word.

"Here." Tommie hands me a bottle of water, and Cassius takes it from him, opens the cap, and sets it in front of me.

"Thanks." It comes out tight from Cassius. He's making me confused. I didn't know he didn't like this male.

"Are there problems?" Tommie leans into the table. Cassius's eye contact accelerates into violence. Carson places a hand on Tommie's back. Caleb stands up, stretches out his back.

"Cash, go for a walk."

"I'm fine."

"No, you're not. He's a guest." Caleb's eyes bleed into Cassius. He's second for a reason. Sometimes he's scary, really really scary.

"The guest needs to understand males don't touch females who aren't wearing red. Do you see any red on her?"

"No."

"Then why did you touch her?" His voice is a coil of rage waiting to unravel.

Cassius stands.

"I'm sorry, I didn't know she was yours." Tommie stays standing, and I see Carson wipe the side of his mouth.

"She's not mine." He sounds frustrated.

"In this pack, if a female isn't wearing red, you can't touch her, no matter how much you want to. Respect their choice." Cassius claims complete control of the conversation. He's all teeth and muscle before Dallas's hand squeezes his brother's shoulder.

"Treajure, let's go dance. Cassius obviously needs to lick his fur down. I'll show you all the moves I've taught him." Caleb has my hand, pulling me up from the table.

"She's not going to dance with you."

"Why? It's not like you're going to ask her to dance, Cash." Caleb's sharp-toothed now. It's rare to see him so pointed, challenging.

Cassius's eyes terrorize his brother's, and I think for a moment they might fight.

"Let's go, Cash." Dallas has a disgruntled growl that shifts Cassius in the opposite direction of his brother.

"I thought he was going to go for your throat," Carson says.

"Me too, but she's worth that fight." Caleb isn't touching me anymore. A distance created. The party is dwindling down. I'm a little drunk; Caleb snuck me a few whiskeys as we cleaned up the mess. He told me it's time for bed when my glasses kept slipping off my face. Cassius went inside a while ago with the twins. He's probably already sleeping.

He comes out of the twins' room. When I step into the hallway away from the stairs, I fidget with my glasses.

"I saw him paw you. I didn't like it." His voice

seems on edge, barely containing something that's making his brow furrow and his hands dig into his pockets.

A sound splits through his throat, bordering on a growl.

"You took your earrings out, and it's hard to follow the rules. Sometimes it gets ahead of me, but if I have to try to follow them, he can too." He sounds strained.

We're close enough now that I can feel the sturdy heat. It's a dependable thing I can lean myself into.

I'm not sure if I heard him right, but my thighs did. They are shaking. I can feel the tremors and the effort it takes to stay standing.

Sometimes it gets ahead of me...

"I'm sorry, Treajure. I'm not good at this. I had this plan, and now, you took those earrings out, and I'm not sure what to do now." His hands dig deeper down into his pockets, held there like a restraint.

"I want to respect you, but I want—" His mouth seals up. He pulls a hand out to scratch at his clean-shaven face before it settles back inside the deep pocket.

"I'm sorry, I'm going to bed before I say or do something stupid. Goodnight." His voice sounds hoarse, heavy. He doesn't close his door all the way; he leaves it open a crack before the bed frame groans with his weight.

I'm left standing in the hallway confused, quiet, and not really understanding everything that has just happened.

Letter 19

Cash,

I can taste the blood in your throat. Stop bleeding for me. I never asked you to bleed for me. That's your own choice, not my choice. Bleed for yourself, not me. I'm fine.

You're going to be fine. Eventually, you're going to be fine. It won't happen overnight, and you will make yourself suffer because that's who you are. You are a sufferer.

I've been watching you, I've been listening to you, I've been thinking about how to help you through all of this, and I think these letters are my the only way to help.

Like I said before, these aren't love letters; these are my thoughts through all of this. It's not meant for you to keep reading them, worship every one of my words; it's meant to read, think, reflect, and move on.

If in the Moon we can look down on the ones we love, know that I won't be looking down on you. I will be waiting to see you again up there, but I am not going to be watching you. I won't be a ghost that can't leave you alone because I can't stay away from the living. I'm not a jilted spirit. I will be at peace when I die.

Don't be afraid to do things because you think I might be watching you. I'm not.

RACHELLE MILLS

Kennedy

218

CHAPTER 20

Lips Feel the Pleasure of Skin

The earrings slip back in.

Cassius has noticed the next day I came downstairs for breakfast. He's noticed all the following weeks with those sidelong glances; he's noticed with those eyes that tell he's wanting to do what red allows. Still, he doesn't act, and it's made me jittery, quick to jump at things, expecting him to be all over me the minute he comes into the house or when I come into his bedroom to sleep.

He'll be on his back, his head turned to me, and ask, "Do you want something, Treajure?" Those times I can't move. I stay stiff in my spot, so he turns himself to the wall. "Goodnight, Specs."

When I'm taking a shower, I expected him to join me or to be standing there when I got out. He doesn't.

A wisp of Cassius's scent lets me know he's been in rooms that I enter. He doesn't look at me, but on occasion, I can see him looking. There is more hunger in his eyes than mine. Still, he doesn't touch me.

I feel as if I am being hunted by him, stalked around the house in a quiet kind of way. This stalking is something that makes my heart pound in my chest and puts my senses on high alert—not from danger, but from wanting to be caught.

I've never been more wanting in my entire life. He's bought a few new things for himself, and he's even started to sing songs on the radio with the kids. I've never seen the edge of his mouth curve up so much.

Drying the dishes, I'm stretching up to put the container on the top shelf, and I feel him behind me taking it out of my hand and stretching up easily to put it away while I'm still on tiptoes. I can feel him breathing right behind me, not moving.

His fingers brush along the corner of my jeans, where the pocket is against my ass.

"Looks like someone needs new jeans." His finger digs into the small hole, skin against skin. I turn my head to look down where his finger is pushed into the hole, his blunt nail scratching at my skin.

"It's been driving me crazy all day."

My breathing is caught off guard.

The hole gets bigger, his finger taking the opportunity of stretching the material to allow it to expand around him. He's now got his finger against the ridge of my panties. He leans into me, his straight nose pressing into the base of my neck. He's inhaling deep with changing breaths.

Something between us is alive. I can feel it like I

feel my own beating heart.

His nail now is clawed, more *Wild* than skin. There is a growl that extends from his chest into my back. It shakes me, not with fear. No, I don't fear this, not him; I could never fear this male standing behind me.

"It's a nice day. I'm going for a run. Would you like to join me? We won't go too far, just up the trail." His nails dig into the pad of my hip, bringing me against his body.

"Say yes."

I nod my head.

"You're going to need to talk to me, Treajure. I know you can make sounds; it's not much different than saying words." My eyes snap to his, and his smile seems naughty. I haven't seen that kind of thing spread wide across his face, a hint of teeth showing. Naughty, mischievous, and so sexy.

He steps away, almost on purpose, I think, and the *Wild* actually whimpers out the noise to him. She doesn't need to be quiet for this male; he's not that man.

"Let her do that again. Let her talk to me." The *Wild* doesn't need me to let her do anything. She whines out again through a throat that is close to atrophy from prolonged non-use.

The sound is rough, painful almost. He doesn't wince away from the noise; he turns me to face him. His blunt nails scratch down my throat, and the *Wild* points her chin to the ceiling, the neck lengthening, letting him scratch at the skin she wants to shift. I can feel the shake of her underneath my skin.

Muscles tense before relaxing to tense out again, pushing against the casing of skin.

She wants out. Now.

"Let's go for a run. Let them meet each other. I've kept him away long enough."

A pause.

"He wants to meet her. I'm going to let him do what he wants to do."

There's a bad shake to my thighs, right above the knees. I'm afraid he's going to notice. If he does, he says nothing.

He's never once mentioned his *Wild* to me, this is the first time, and what's inside me is rejoicing in a fit of silent yips and tail chasing.

She's wildly enthusiastic to meet him as well. Too enthusiastic.

He goes to the back mudroom first. I can hear him peel all the layers off him before the back door opens. My turn to take everything off, including the earrings and glasses. I come out in a flowered robe; I think it might be silk. I've never felt something so light and smooth before. I'm almost blind except for the blurs of shapes.

"Ready?" He turns and shifts really fast; the cocoon of skin releases to the body of the *Wild,* who faces the forest. Discarding the robe, my turn to shift, and she only sees in blurred shapes as if cataracts are over her eyes.

There is a nudge to our flank, a sniff of our mouth, more sniffs to our underbelly, our female parts. The *Wild* does the same with him, sniffs him up and down, and all around. He's a meaty male with a height to him.

The *Wild* follows the male's lead. He takes a gentle route, not demanding anything of her non-existent skill level.

He keeps nudging her flank, letting his body slide along hers. He nips into her haunch, and she nips him back with teeth that don't draw blood, more gums than teeth.

There is no running full out; the path is even, without dips or hills. She's steady on her feet until the male starts to become playful and upends her. He holds, rushes her, then pulls back at the last minute. When she rights herself, he's there as a big blur on hind legs to pounce back on her. She plays back, full of her strength that doesn't match his.

They roll on the ground together and lick at their mouths and inside of their jowls. They explore the other's body without any kind of restraint until the male gets a hold of the *Wild's* neck.

He holds her with powerful jaws. He could take her throat. He could kill her if he wanted to.

A whine from the *Wild* before she tries to push her neck inside teeth that have her wanting to be bitten.

There is no hesitation before the bite is felt; it's a solid, clean, through the skin kind of bite that has her back legs give out.

The *Wild* experiences complete paralysis of the body from pure uninhibited pleasure. Teeth retract and she lays on her side, panting open-mouthed, tongue hanging out.

He gives her a few moments before trying to get her to her feet. She licks the side of his face, and he stretches his neck out, practically shoving it between the *Wild's* teeth.

There is no hesitation with her, she clamps down, and the surge of him is felt, a complete overwhelming shift of my internal makeup. It makes room for something else within, some other presences that shift along the bone line that intertwines within my private spaces. The marrow of my bones expand as Cassius is felt within.

I feel internally swollen, everything is excessive, and it's hard to pick my head up. There's a need to shift from fur to skin.

Something besides me is inside my head. I can feel the strange presence taking up space just on the peripheral edge.

He shakes himself out, a lick to the side of my neck, cheek pressed against cheek, before he stretches and waits for the *Wild* to find her legs again.

When his *Wild* tries to mount her, she tucks her tail around her, the nip is real this time, and Cassius sheds his fur to skin. He's a blur.

"He got ahead of me. My apologies." Now his hand runs down her neck, scratches at her flank; she rolls on her back, belly exposed, and he laughs.

"It was the right thing to do, Treajure. I hope you aren't upset?" I can't see him real good, nothing but an outline of a body. The *Wild* whines in her throat; he touches her cheek with his, and kisses her neck, her throat, and licks off the blood in her fur.

He shifts again and walks slowly, almost reluctantly back to the house. He goes inside first. I find the robe and shift quickly, putting it on me. I still can't see, and I can hear him dressing in the

CASSIUS

layers of himself.

I can feel his fingers at one of my ears. He pushes the earring through the hole. I feel the deliberate way he touches the back of my ear; it gives me a shiver in my spine.

"That feels good when I touch you there." I can't even shake my head, because he's pushing the other earring through the hole, securing it with the backing. The pad of his thumb plays with the thin skin behind my ear for a few staggering moments. I can feel something rush through my blood, but it's not my blood rushing. It's his.

My glasses are put on by him next after I blink a few times, and his eyes are waiting for mine to see him.

"Perfect."

My breath is gone.

His nose runs the length of mine, slow.

Everything responds—my body leans into his.

He takes a minute before those lips are on mine.

Soft. Warm. Gentle.

I want to take a taste of his tongue that is nudging between my lips.

He breathes in, heavy. I can feel him curl his shoulders around my body. I'm being pulled flush to his chest.

He's a force...

This is urgent male; he kisses with ownership. To claim my lips as his, only his. His tongue belongs against my tongue.

The warmth inside me spreads, and he makes this noise that he kisses me through. Our breaths meet and are inhaled by the other.

225

"Tell me your name," he asks through the break in his lips still pressed to mine. "Let me know your name." He's on my mouth again, eyes closed. His hands run back down my robe to mid-thigh, lifting it up next time as he runs them back up me. I can feel the cold air hitting my inner thighs as that throbbing heat spreads deeper below my mound.

He's stone-hard; I can feel him. He's responding the same as me—I'm as slick as he is hard.

I have no underwear on, and I can feel the wetness with each clench of my thighs.

His hips shift, and I can't help the moan that comes from deep in my throat. He stiffens.

"Do it again." The noise is made again, and he rewards me with a kiss that demands I give him everything back he's giving me. He pulls me even closer with a drawn-out noise from his chest.

We're both breathing hard. His hand skims over the front of my thighs to reach around and grip me by the ass, picking me up so I can feel him on my mound. I feel the length of him straining through his jeans, pushing into my space.

Heart pounding each time my hips shift into his.

I can barely breathe; everything is a rush forward.

My hips desperately push back into his. We are lips and tongues, hands, and I can't stop from thinking I'd like nothing more than to shove his jeans to his ankles and feel a male for the first time in my mouth.

A raspy breath drags out of his lungs as his hand smooths down over the silk robe against my mound, and I freeze.

The back door opens, and instead of jumping away, he holds me to him, our foreheads touching. I'm embarrassed to be caught but not him. He makes no move to hide this from anyone.

"Sorry." The Luna backs out, but not before the twins bully themselves past her.

"What are you doing?" Ken asks his father.

"I'm giving Treajure a kiss. Is that okay?"

"I guess so." Ken makes a disgusted face, and Dee's eyes are as big as mine.

"Why?" Dee asks.

"Because I like her." He pulls away his eyes from mine to meet the twins, then to his mother, whose face has become red and blotchy.

"Why do you like her?" Ken is persistent and confused.

"I just do."

"I like her too," Dee chimes in and holds my hand.

"I like her too," Ken mimics his sister's reply.

"Well, it's settled, we all like you." I can hear the smile through Cassius's voice.

"We all like her," the voice of the Luna joins in, and before I know it, I have to take my glasses off and wipe away the tears that keep coming from what I feel inside me. Joy.

Letter 20

Cash,
You should move on because I already have.
Kennedy

CHAPTER 21

Skin in the Shade of Slate Drawn on Paper

Cassius's range is wide. I can feel his eye on my face even if I can't see him. I feel every glance; I feel every brush of vision that keeps coming back to my face, to my lips, to my neck. I feel him, the security of the inside of him.

"Well. I think I'm going to bed. Goodnight. Are you coming, Grace?" I understand where Cassius gets his puppy pout; the Silverback looks at the Luna all lip and desire with eyes that grow big. The Luna nods her head, and if he was in *Wild* form, his tail would be wagging incessantly. He has a little pepper in his step as he make his way the other side of the house.

"Well, goodnight, see you in the morning." His mother kisses his forehead, then she presses her lips against mine.

"Treajure, I'd like to talk to you." He doesn't mumble; his words are clear precision. "I want to ask you if it would be all right if I marked you?"

I stiffen slightly.

"Not today." He shows me his palms. He's calm.

"I'm just asking if it would be all right if I marked you, only if you want me to. I know the *Wilds* have done their business, and now it's time for us. You and me."

My legs buckle, and I'm sitting on the chair, all loose as if I don't own a bone in my body. Cassius waits for an answer.

"You're going to have to tell me what you want. I won't do it without you telling me, Treajure. I know you can talk. I can feel all those words inside you." He touches his chest with his hand, the center of him.

"I promise I won't do anything you aren't ready for. We'll take all this slow. As slow as you need." His eyes are trained sharp right on my face before they soften, and I swear he's smiling through them now.

"I'm off to bed. Goodnight, Specs." He doesn't kiss my forehead; he brushes his lips on mine before pulling away with a subtle growl that terrorizes the deepness of my sex.

He leaves his door cracked slightly, and I can hear him get on top of his bed. It's dark in his room except for the sickle moon that is out.

Entering, I stop in the middle of his room. The outline of his body is held still on his bed. I'm not sure he's breathing, but I can feel the race of him.

His head turns toward me. "Do you want something, Treajure?" His voice reaches out, touches my face. I can feel it all over me, surrounding me, holding me like a warm blanket.

There is no answer from me. The word *you* is trapped the same way spit is under my tongue and it's swallowed down, leaving me there standing by myself with everything surrounding me.

"Goodnight, Specs." Cassius rolls on his side, facing the wall, his back to me, and I slip underneath his bed, feeling the wooden frame above me until my breathing is even and my eyes can't stay open any longer.

The next morning has Cassius working on his computer, but he makes it a point to get up from the table to kiss me good morning in front of everyone. The Silverback takes a sip of his coffee with a toothy grin stretched as wide as his shirt across his face.

The twins just stare at their father, at me, and start to giggle.

"Nothing's wrong with kissing," the Alpha says with an even brighter smile glued to his face.

"That's right, nothing is wrong with kissing." Luna Grace wraps her arms around her mate's chest and kisses him on the cheek.

"Now Grace, you've made my lips jealous, and you know we can't have that, can we?"

"You're right, forgive me, Alpha." Her lips touch his, long and slow, not indecent but there is a fine line.

"Better?" She pulls away, and his neck follows her lips.

"Almost." He kisses her once more, a little deeper, and Cassius looks away, the twins giggle, and I turn red.

"Better. Them lips are a jealous thing, Grace.

You know better than to start with the cheek." His teeth nip at her neck before he leans back against the chair.

Crane gags.

His mother throws a butter knife at his head, misses, and Caleb smacks him lightly.

"What did I do?" Crane asks.

"You made your mother mad."

"And you've never?"

"That was when I was younger. I'm a changed wolf." Caleb's teeth shine white toward Crane.

Crane huffs, "Don't you have your own house?"

"The food's better here." Caleb opens the fridge and helps himself.

"When you're older, Crane, you'll understand." I can see the way Crane's skin crawls as Caleb pops a few grapes in his mouth, teeth smiling as he chews.

Crane stretches out his shoulders, squaring himself against his brother, and Caleb stretches himself to his completed height—a big wolf who knows it.

"Outside." A quick whip of a word comes from the Alpha.

"He started it." Crane points, and Caleb is right there with a pulled-out bottom lip that tremors as if he's going to cry, teasing his brother.

Crane chases Caleb outside, and I can see them wrestling on the ground. Ken jumps from his seat and goes outside, jumping on the pile of them with his elbow.

Dee rolls her eyes. "Boys." And for her, that says it all, but she does get off her chair and runs outside to throw her own elbows into Caleb's chest. He

231

grunts and groans, holding his heart in pain. Crane lets Ken toss him around and fakes injuries as they bite and nip each other with blunt teeth and no claws.

Cassius runs outside and tackles his brother hard to the ground. It's rough but gentle, and the Alpha even gets in on it.

The sketchbook sits beside the laptop, and I take the opportunity to open it. The noise that comes out of my chest startles even me.

The first page is me, in a shadowed sort of way; all I can make out are my glasses on a blur of a face. The next picture is more my eyes through the glasses. Each page different, each page getting clearer and sharper.

I can't stop the desperate flip of each page. Everything is here, all the details I never knew I had. Each picture a picture in itself, it tells some kind of out of focus story. The middle of the book has my body now drawn with a face that's becoming clearer. More light than shade now. I'm becoming clearer with each line the pencil makes.

Another desperate flip, I want to ingrain this into my memory forever.

A clear portrait of me, a side view of my face, the ruby earring is the only thing that holds color in the entire book. Everything else is shades of slate.

A throat clears, and my head lifts from the book, dropping it on the table. Hands tremble.

Cassius stares right into me, and I feel that everything is about to change.

The quiet seems solemn and heavy.

Everything will change…

CHAPTER 22

Paper Dreams in the Form of Solid Flesh

Every night Cassius asks me, "Do you want something, Treajure?" Every night I say the same thing, nothing, and he does the same thing, turning on his side facing the wall, wishing me *goodnight*.

The days are filled with hugs and kisses, deep kisses that have his hands all over me, and my hands all over him, but that's where it stops, and I'm about to go mad with want.

Tonight's no different. He's on his bed fully clothed; the layers of him are all there. His head turns, the full moon's light reflecting in his eyes.

"Do you want something, Treajure?"

This time, I make a noise in my throat to prepare the muscles to work.

Breathe...

His whole body turns toward me nice and slow.

"Cassius." It croaks out, but out it comes. I clear my throat again and this time say his name better than the first time.

233

It takes him a minute to sit up then stand to make his way over to me.

Everything changes. I can feel it inside him, inside me.

"Say it again."

He turns his ear to me, and I reach up on tiptoes to press his name against his ear. "Cassius."

Can he feel me trembling? Because when I put my hand on his chest to undo the first few buttons on his shirt, I can feel the shifting of his skin.

The weight of his hands are on the pad of my hips. He watches my fingers as I unbutton every button his shirt has before pulling it down off his shoulders, and past his arms, and finally his wrists. A layer of him lays at our feet.

"It's only fair." He shifts his eyes to meet mine before the shirt I wear is pulled off my body.

A layer leaves my skin.

His t-shirt is soft in my hands when I pull it off him, letting my knuckles touch his torso, his chest, shoulders, and finally the shirt is off.

He grunts through a flared nose.

The palms of my hands run up and down his back before the nails dig in against the shifting meat of his muscles.

He holds my bottom lip with his teeth, not too hard, but enough that I can't pull away from him as his hand holds an appreciation of lace. He strokes the material with his thumb, rubbing against the nipple that feels too tight.

He makes a low, urgent noise; his hand fills with my breast, a firm squeeze before the skin of him dips inside the cup, feeling me raw without the lace between us.

That draws out a noise from deep within, a moan that he swallows down in a giant gulp.

I feel up his spine. His shoulders are curled around me. I feel the skin along his neck to the new growth of hair that I scratch my fingers into.

Heat flushes, rushes, and consumes all thoughts.

My thighs clench when he holds the other breast in his hand. I sigh, muscles shift, tense but not relaxed.

"You're perfect," he says into my neck, teeth scraping at the skin.

Everything is changing...

I feel him through his jeans. He's ready, hard and bulging. I'm slick—I can feel myself soaking through my underwear.

Undoing the button, he dips his head to watch my fingers. The zipper pulls down. I can't hear it over my breathing. I look up at him as I pull those jeans down his hips, past his thighs, and leave them at his ankles.

Cassius has pulled his bottom lip into his mouth, and he's all eyes now. His chest heaves, and I place a kiss against the stone rod of him through the material of his underwear.

Fingers hook to the band of his boxers.

"Are you sure?" His hand touches my cheek. "You don't have to."

Cassius doesn't understand, I need to.

My knees hit the carpet, and as I go down, his boxers come down to his ankles. He steps out of his clothes and pulls a hiss of breath in when I run my nose along his length, inhaling his scent.

There's some sort of primal smell to his sex that goads me on, that makes me want to taste him with my tongue. I can feel the saliva pool in the back of my throat. I want him inside my mouth.

His knees bend when I lick the tip of him, tasting that fluid that starts to bead from his hole.

I can feel his fingers weave through my hair when I sink my mouth down on him, putting him halfway in, feeling the smoothness of his balls, before grasping the base of him.

"Fuck." The sound crawls out of him.

He doesn't fit all the way inside, but I try my best, and for my effort, he's letting his sound rumble around the room.

He lets me explore him without interference, and I explore the male side of him. Licking the underside of his shaft, working my tongue around the shine of his head. Exploring his balls, feeling how they move in my hand.

A hard breath comes out of his mouth when I stroke him from the base, my mouth around the tip. His fingers dig into my hair, borderline painful.

His hips are moving now, I can feel him watching what I'm doing, and I cast my eyes up with him in my open mouth.

"Fuck." His legs bend a little more, he thrusts himself inside the space of my mouth, and I gag from it.

Eyes water.

"It's only fair," he says through exposed teeth, bringing me up to my feet.

He groans when the zipper of my pants come down, he inhales when the material pulls down from my thighs, he takes them off completely, and he pauses to go on his knees.

His straight nose pushes into my mound; his tongue, oh, I can feel his tongue right there, licking me through the material.

He looks up at me with something precious written across his face. His tongue drags down the curve of my underwear. He groans with half-closed eyes. Nails dig into my thighs, holding me still, and all I want to do is shove myself in his face.

I can't stop looking down at him even when his fingers curl around the band of my underwear, pulling them down, and that tongue hits a nerve that makes me jump from the sheer force of pleasure.

The bones in my legs feel like they're turning from solid into a liquid. I hold onto his head as that tongue fleshes out the noise in my chest. I hold onto him until my knees start to bend and my hips try to curl around his face.

He pulls me closer to him, spreading me with the flat part of his tongue.

It's just too much, and before I sink completely down, I'm lifted up, put on his bed. He crawls between my legs with hungry eyes, his teeth dragging his bottom lip in with a groan. His shoulders spread my legs wider as he nudges himself into my space, my private space that no one has entered before.

It's getting harder to breathe; I can't feel the mattress against my back anymore. I try to curl around his head, and the flat part of his hand pushes into my belly to flatten me back out.

A gasp when he licks me harder as his finger

enters me. One finger and it's enough to make me want to come.

He spreads me wider, and the growl spreads through his chest. A moan comes from mine. It's hard to think about anything else but that tongue circling around my womanhood, his mouth sucking it in, his tongue teasing it with small strokes. He adds another finger, and I feel the pressure of it, a small whimper that turns into a moan once I get used to the feeling of having something substantial inside me.

I can feel myself, oh, I can feel the tightening of my inner walls, and he pulls those fingers out and his tongue away. Panic comes from my lips. He's not going to stop, is he?

He's all flushed when he climbs up me, his mouth goes over mine, and I can taste myself on his lips. This feels perversely intimate, as if he's sharing something special with me, and I'm sharing myself with him.

The feel of his stone-hard cock pressing into my mound drives me to shift my hips and spread my legs so he can settle the weight of him there. He's on my neck, teeth scraping down the flesh. I can feel the lines that are left behind from the push of the points that are going deeper into the flesh, just not breaking through it.

I want them to break through, pierce me. I clench, thinking of the feeling of what it will be like. He's pulled down each strap of my bra, unfastening it before laying my back against the mattress. He takes it off nice and slow, his head bent kissing my chest, kissing my neck, kissing my shoulders, back up to my mouth. His fingertip runs circles around my nipples, getting them worked up; the skin gathers all up and puckers tight. Painful almost, but his mouth is there to suck one of them inside. He's all wet, and when he pulls away, he leaves a shine to the one. He explores the other, just as delicate.

"Have you ever done this before?" There is no judgment in his eyes.

I shake my head no.

His eyes half close, and before I know it, he starts to kiss me again, all urgent and hungry. His hand cups my breast again, and I lean my chest into him, wanting that hand to go right to the bones of me.

He grinds himself against my mound; the pressure is everything.

His thighs spread my legs as he centers himself to my center.

Cassius is all long-toothed now, and he's staring at my neck. The skin of him is shifting underneath my palms, tensing, and I close my eyes, shut them up real tight, waiting.

Nothing happens…

"There's no reason to be scared. I'm going to try not to hurt you." He slides us into a sitting position, and my spread thighs wrap around his waist, his stone-hard shaft between us.

Dark pupils expand into the blue irises, taking control of his vision.

"You are mine." His teeth scrape down my neck. His voice lingers against my throat. The breath in my throat shortens into a little gasps of tight air.

"You are my hope." Teeth push in deeper to the hollow of my neck, voice rough and raw sounding from his throat. His tongue slides out and meets my naked flesh, licking at the spot.

My body begs for the feel of teeth in me; my neck arches and lengthens as his straight nose inhales against my skin.

"My love." He exhales out. He's all teeth now. I can feel his body shifting in the form of skin and fur. Combing himself into one form.

He lifts me by my ass, and I can feel the head of his shaft press into my entrance. He shifts his hips and kisses me again, with some kind of hunger that is barely controlled.

He sinks my hips down on him slowly, and there is a stretch that takes my breath right out of my lungs. His mouth is there breathing into me, filling my lungs up, forcing me to exhale out as he opens me up.

Cassius shifts up, and I am moved down in one movement that has me clinging onto my bottom lip with teeth. His tongue is there, to take my teeth away from my bottom lip. He lets his tongue swipe at my mouth, and I let my tongue swipe into his.

"My light." Words on his lips press into mine.

Eye to eye.

We are joined. I'm not sure where he ends and I begin.

I take all of him to the base, and it fills tight, and the stretch hurts, but not as bad as I thought it would be; this is a different kind of hurt. Needed pain.

"My weakness," his voice breaks through my moan.

He finally moves, and the way he does, it's like he was meant to be inside me, shifting himself in and out. My hips start to move with his; again teeth scrape along the line of my throat. Digging in, hard, splitting the skin now.

He keeps moving inside me, pulling out, pushing in, while those teeth tease my flesh.

I'm holding onto his shoulders that are strong and dependable.

We make love on his lap.

"My strength." His breath is quick. He lets out a gasp that's held long after the words have come out.

I hold his face in my hands now, wanting to see him, wanting to see the desire he has for me. He can't put those teeth away. He's breathing hard with every push inside; I'm getting so close. I didn't know it could be like this. I had expectations, but this, this was beyond what I thought it would be like.

He's deeper than I thought possible; I'm stretched all around him. There is no space inside me left. He's occupied it all.

He grinds himself inside me, pulls almost out, shoves back in. His tongue on mine, his hands all over me, he's all breath and I am following his lead.

Again, his teeth find my throat, and I arch my neck to the side, allowing him to take it if he wants.

Take my throat, I want to scream, *take everything from me, I want to give you it all.*

The points are the first to be felt, he's moving faster inside me, and he bites down, hard, and I can't breathe…

He groans, grunts, and stiffens underneath me,

pushing himself so deep that I can't help myself from clenching all around him, trying to bring him into me more. My insides are milking what's coming out of him.

This is blinding pleasure, where everything stops but what's happening inside.

I can feel him pulsing within, each jerk of his shaft expelling his seed into me. I can feel it running out of me, and he continues and continues to come, and so do I.

Teeth retract; the flat part of his tongue licks at my neck until he's satisfied with something.

My back presses against the mattress now. He hasn't slipped out. He's staying locked within my space.

I don't want to move. His weight is a comfort, security.

"You're okay?"

I want to ask him the same question, but I only nod my head yes.

"That was amazing." He presses his mouth to mine. "Thank you." Another press of lips to mouth.

"I'm going to love you the way you should be." Another kiss.

"I've been in love with you for a while, and I won't lie—it scared me." His hips shift, and he's still as hard as he was before I pulled down his pants.

"I needed to change before all of this." He shifts his hips again, and I take the fullness of him between my spread legs.

I can feel the point of my teeth; I can feel the *Wild's* urgent need to mark him, to claim this male and make him hers, and I want to claim him. I want to put my mark on him and let everyone know he belongs to me.

His hand grips my waist as he pushes deeper inside, dragging himself out, pushing in.

"I don't want to stop. I'm not ready to get out of you. Not yet." My toes curl because he's rubbing into the spot that makes me feel everything.

"I can hear you in my head. I can hear your voice." There is a rush of his voice all over my tender neck.

My heel is running up the back of his thigh to push into his ass so he goes deeper.

He lifts his head and groans low, neck exposed.

"You have a beautiful voice, Sabe."

For the longest time, that's what we do, my name on repeat coming from his throat while he fills me and I try to hold him inside every time his shafts drags down before pushing back inside. Like a game of chase and hold. Our chests pushed flush together.

The mattress has too much give and he's sinking me into it with every drive of his shaft. He's becoming more insistent, more demanding on how I am taking him inside me. I spread my legs more, and my teeth draw blood from my bottom lip. He licks at it, cleaning me.

I moan with each hard thrust that digs in deep, filling me, stretching the inside.

His neck is there, right there, the hollow part where the skin on the bone dips down, and I know what to do, like instinct.

Teeth dig in point first, and I can feel him stiffen.

His weight drops on my body, and he's holding onto me, like something inside him is breaking apart while the inside of me becomes full.

Again my edge is reached, and this time I need to hold onto him just as much as he's holding onto me.

Things are starting to fit together, weave into some kind of hardened structure that we now share together.

Everything changes. We hold ourselves together, clinging to the other as we drown then breathe finally together.

I want to tell him how much I love him, but the words are still stuck, and I'm afraid they might always be.

"It's all right. I hear you now. I can hear you, Sabe."

He tucks me into his chest with the words *I love you* pressed against my ear.

When I open my eyes back up, the sun has just come up, and I'm still wrapped up in his arms, held secure and with love.

I am loved.

Everything has changed.

ACKNOWLEDGEMENTS

I need to thank Cal for giving me the encouragement I needed to get the story finished. You are a true soulful light.

ABOUT THE AUTHOR

Rachelle Mills lives in Canada with her family and two dogs. She's a lover of all things that have to do with Nature and Wildlife.

Mills has won acclaim from readers for her fantastically realized paranormal werewolf universes, where alpha males fight tooth and claw and society – more often than not – is determined to make the path of true love as rocky and uncomfortable as possible.

Her rich, paranormal universe is packed with characters that frustrate and enthrall readers with an expert grasp of the complexities of the primal fight that werewolves have; their human, controlled side, and the vicious, ugly, and virtually untamable were-side which can leave a trail of destruction in its wake.

Mills' writing style is charged with emotion and richly descriptive, bringing the universe of her often-gritty stories into vivid life.

SOCIAL MEDIA LINKS

Facebook:
https://www.facebook.com/Rachelle-Mills-298700590732805/?ref=bookmarks

Twitter:
https://twitter.com/whiskeyqueenn?lang=en

Goodreads:
https://www.goodreads.com/author/show/14827762.Rachelle_Mills

Instagram:
https://www.instagram.com/whiskeyqueenn/

Join our Reader Group on Facebook and
don't miss out on meeting our authors and
entering epic giveaways!

Join today! *"Where reading a book is your
first step to becoming limitless..."*

**https://www.facebook.com/groups/Limitle
ssReading/**

CPSIA information can be obtained
at www.ICGtesting.com
Printed in the USA
LVHW041125111119
636959LV00006B/2086

9 781640 347885